The Island Clinic

Saving lives in St. Victoria!

Welcome to paradise! Or, as it's officially known,
the Caribbean island of St. Victoria—
home to chief of staff Nate Edwards and his private
hospital, The Island Clinic. With the motto
"We are *always* here to help," The Island Clinic
was created as both a safe haven for the
rich and famous to receive medical treatment
and a lifeline for the local community.

This summer, we're going to meet
The Island Clinic's medical team as they work hard
to save lives…and, just maybe, get a shot at love!

How to Win the Surgeon's Heart
by Tina Beckett

Caribbean Paradise, Miracle Family
by Julie Danvers

Available now!

...atrician

...ost Nurse
by Charlotte...kes

Coming soon!

Dear Reader,

Have you ever felt uncertain about what the future holds? I think most of us have at some time or other. Sometimes those fears can consume us…paralyze us. That's the spot surgeon Sasha James finds herself in. She has finally put a failed relationship behind her and now has her future all mapped out. But you know how that goes, right? Trouble arrives, in the form of life events and, more importantly, a man she'll have to work closely with for the next several weeks. A man who makes her insides go all wonky.

Thank you for joining Sasha and Nate as they struggle to free themselves from their pasts once and for all. And maybe, just maybe, this special couple will find a little something extra along the way. I hope you enjoy reading their story as much as I loved writing it. These two characters stayed with me long after I typed "The End."

I have to say working with Julie Danvers, Annie O'Neil and Charlotte Hawkes on The Island Clinic continuity was a dream come true. I can't wait for you to read their stories and get a taste of paradise!

Much love,

Tina Beckett

HOW TO WIN
THE SURGEON'S HEART

TINA BECKETT

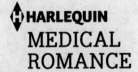

Special thanks and acknowledgment are given to Tina Beckett
for her contribution to The Island Clinic miniseries.

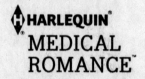

HARLEQUIN®
MEDICAL
ROMANCE™

Recycling programs
for this product may
not exist in your area.

ISBN-13: 978-1-335-40863-1

How to Win the Surgeon's Heart

Copyright © 2021 by Harlequin Books S.A.

This edition published by arrangement with Harlequin Books S.A.

For questions and comments about the quality of this book,
please contact us at CustomerService@Harlequin.com.

Harlequin Enterprises ULC
22 Adelaide St. West, 40th Floor
Toronto, Ontario M5H 4E3, Canada
www.Harlequin.com

Printed in U.S.A.

Three-times Golden Heart® Award finalist **Tina Beckett** learned to pack her suitcases almost before she learned to read. Born to a military family, she has lived in the United States, Puerto Rico, Portugal and Brazil. In addition to traveling, Tina loves to cuddle with her pug, Alex, spend time with her family and hit the trails on her horse. Learn more about Tina from her website or "friend" her on Facebook.

Books by Tina Beckett

Harlequin Medical Romance

New York Bachelor's Club

Consequences of Their New York Night
The Trouble with the Tempting Doc

A Summer in São Paulo

One Hot Night with Dr. Cardoza

A Family to Heal His Heart
A Christmas Kiss with Her Ex-Army Doc
Risking It All for the Children's Doc
It Started with a Winter Kiss

Visit the Author Profile page
at Harlequin.com for more titles.

To my kids for always supporting me. I love you!

PROLOGUE

NATE EDWARDS STOOD on the tarmac, a tiny cloth doll clutched in his hand, awaiting the Medicine Around the World plane that would whisk him away from Saint Victoria and the aftermath of the hurricane that had wreaked havoc on the small Caribbean island. His thumb rubbed across the doll's rough cloth, trying not to picture the tearstained eyes of her parents as they presented the gift to him. But their faces were forever burned into his memory. As was the dark-haired child who had been so very sick. And yet she'd managed the tiniest of smiles for him. With the island's hospital obliterated by the fury of the storm, there had been little hope of saving her.

But God, how he'd wanted to. How he'd fought for her.

The phone in his pocket pinged.

Hell. His team had had only the most rudimentary supplies to work with during their stay. How, then, could cell phone signals still get through?

He pulled the phone out of his pocket, glad he'd charged it before packing for the trip home.

His mom's name appeared at the top of the screen.

Glad you're coming home today. We have a big surprise waiting for you! Your father and I can't wait for you to see it.

A sense of dread filled his gut. He'd hoped by coming to the island he could circumvent their plans and buy himself a little more time to explain things to them. And then there was Tara, who had been hinting about settling down once he finished specializing. Except so much had changed. He tucked the doll under his arm as a bead of sweat rolled down his temple. He typed back.

Please don't do anything until I get there.

He had no idea how he was going to tell them that he had no intention of joining their practice. After his trip to Saint Victoria—which they hadn't approved of—the last thing he wanted to do was practice plastic surgery on the rich and famous.

One of his colleagues came up beside him. "Nate, we just got the results back on your patient's mystery illness."

Too late. Marie had already passed away. Still he forced himself to ask. "What was it?"

"Schistosomiasis. It must have damaged her liver and intestines beyond repair. That's why she was so jaundiced. She had to have had it for a while."

A parasite found in water had killed her? He closed his eyes. That possibility had never even crossed his mind. They'd had to send samples via water courier to a neighboring island, but he'd known in his heart it was too late. It should make him feel better to know there was nothing he could have done. Instead he just felt…empty. And now he had to go home and face his parents and Tara.

He forced himself to meet the eyes of his colleague. "Thanks for letting me know."

"You're welcome." Peter clapped him on the back. "Not your fault."

"Thanks."

What else could he say?

Just then his phone pinged again, the screen lighting up and drawing his attention to the words that were printed there.

Too late. It's already done.

Three smiley faces appeared at the end of the phrase.

She was right. It was already done. All of it.

Marie. This trip. His decision about what to do with his future.

Maybe Tara would understand. Maybe she'd even want to join him.

He stuffed his phone back in his pocket and cradled the worn doll in his palms.

Because he was coming back to this island, someday, and he was going to use his training to do something good. Something worthwhile.

If it took every penny he had.

CHAPTER ONE

SASHA JAMES GROUND her teeth as she waited for the shuttle that connected The Island Clinic with Saint Victoria Hospital. She was surprised the man hadn't taken his fancy helicopter instead. After all, he was the one who'd paid for Saint Victoria Hospital to have the helipad installed. And for The Island Clinic's. His own little kingdom.

"Not fair, Sash. You know good and well he's done a lot for the island over the last three years."

But how long before he got bored with playing the part of a philanthropist?

She rolled her eyes. It would not do to make an enemy of the man, because without a doubt, she would come out on the losing end. Everyone she'd talked to idolized him.

Especially those wealthy women who had vacation homes here on the island. There were rumors that some of them had their eyes set on dating him. That a few might have done just that. Except the clinic's chief of staff was apparently not interested in deeper relationships.

Sound familiar?

The shuttle, with The Island Clinic's picture emblazoned on the side, pulled up to the doors of the hospital's main entrance. Why had she been appointed as the one to meet Mr. Big Wig?

Because they were short staffed and Sasha had no immediate surgeries scheduled. Basically, she'd drawn the short straw. It was also why Dr. Edwards had offered to come over from the clinic.

The door to the back opened and a couple of people got off the shuttle, followed by a man who must be Edwards in black jeans and a matching polo shirt.

She'd expected Armani and had gotten *Men in Black*, instead. Great.

Maybe he'd decided to dress down for the Saint Victoria crowd.

There she went again.

Pushing through the glass door, the heat outside swept across her cheeks and made her clothing want to stick to her skin. She hurried to meet him halfway down the sidewalk. "Dr. Edwards? I'm Sasha James. Nice to meet you."

"You, as well."

A quick smile appeared, forming a crease on the left side of his face, one which disappeared in the blink of an eye. With black hair swept back from a strong forehead and an even stronger chin, the man's features were swoon-worthy. Fortunately, Sasha was no swooner. Not anymore. Her gaze traveled a little further down, where the swell of biceps was noticeable under the sleeves of his knit shirt. How in the world had he gotten those? Warmth washed through her belly, and her hand instinctively went there to push back the tide. It didn't work.

She had to admit his appearance didn't immediately scream wealth and privilege, the way she'd expected it to. The way Austin's had done. There was no softness to his jawline, no paunch around his middle—not that her former boyfriend had had either of those things. Maybe, like Austin, this man spent hours exercising to keep himself fit. But she didn't think so, and underneath that rugged veneer there was something that said this was a man not to be trifled with.

Well, that was okay. She'd already met his type during her time at Harvard. Rich men were a dime a dozen there. And they were not always who they seemed, as she'd discovered.

She had to admit though, Dr. Edwards had done quite a bit for the island, had taken in a lot of Saint Victoria's hardship cases. Courtesy of The Island Clinic's wealthy clientele.

Okay, now that she had Dr. Edwards, she wasn't quite sure what to do with him. And she'd been too peeved by the request to meet him to ask. "Did you know where they wanted you?"

"Wherever you need me."

Her palm pressed even harder against her abdomen as the graveled tones turned the burner up on whatever was happening inside her.

"Dr. Edwards, I think—"

"Nate. Please."

She didn't want to call him Nate. Didn't want to be on a first-name basis with the man, despite the fact that she called almost everyone else by their given name. This just seemed…different. "I think I'll stick to Dr. Edwards if it's okay with you."

He lifted his shoulders in an easy shrug, although she was pretty sure there was a tension to the movement that hadn't been there moments earlier. "That's fine… *Dr.* James."

His lips curved as he added her title, making her realize how strange she was acting.

But it wasn't an act. She had no idea why he was even here. What could he do, exactly? Did he practice actual medicine anymore? Or was he just a showpiece for the clinic?

"Marcus…er… Dr. Warren," too late she realized she'd used the other doctor's name making a mockery of her reticence to calling him Nate, "worked in the ER. It's where our biggest shortage of staff is. If you're up to it."

"I'll do my best to keep up." Again that smile rolled across his face, that crease making her shiver. Was he making fun of her?

Her hand finally dropped from her stomach and curled into a ball next to her hip. "I'll walk you over, since I'm helping out there, as well." Today was her scheduled day off, but there was no way she was going to sit at home while everyone else in the ER struggled to cope.

"Thanks, I appreciate that."

In silence, they walked down the tiled corridor toward the small hospital's emergency room. Dr. Edwards threw her a look.

"What?"

"Nothing." His smile this time was a bit cooler than it had been. "How long have you been at the hospital?"

"A little over three years."

"Do you specialize?"

That made her hackles rise all over again. "I'm a surgeon, so yes. Why?" Did it matter to him what she did? If so, she might not be able to refrain from giving him the "we're all equal here" speech that she'd had to give to more than one person over the last couple of years.

"No reason. I just don't think we've met before, and I thought I knew most of the staff over here."

She didn't tell him that she made herself scarce whenever she heard that Nate Edwards was coming over to the hospital. She hadn't realized how much she'd prejudged him until right this moment though. Everyone she knew always spoke of him as if he could do no wrong. Maybe that was why. It had rubbed her up the wrong way, somehow. The man was not a god. He was a mortal just like everyone else.

But where she'd expected to meet an abrupt, pompous ass who thought he was better than everyone else, she was seeing something different. Either the man was a good actor…or he wasn't as much of a jerk as she'd painted in her head. She wasn't sure if that was a good thing or bad.

She'd give him the benefit of the doubt. For now. But she was going to reserve final judgment until she saw how he was with actual patients. The island's population, that is—not the wealthy ones from his fancy clinic.

"I don't think we have met. I'm in surgery quite a bit, so we've obviously missed each other." It was true, but she was well aware of the fact that she was fudging it just a bit. He was at the hospital once every week or so, normally to pick up a patient or check on one who had been discharged back to Saint Victoria Hospital.

"Obviously."

The way he said it made her squirm, as if he was glad not to have met her before this. Was she being that unfair? She wasn't trying to be.

Wasn't she? Didn't she guard her heart a lot more now that she was older and wiser?

They arrived at the ER to a chaotic scene. An ambulance had just pulled into the bay. Sasha glanced around and didn't see any other doctors. "I'll help with whatever's going on here, if you want to check in."

"Checking in can wait. I'll see if they need a hand."

They both hurried over to where the EMTs were sliding a gurney out of the ambulance.

"What have you got?" she asked.

"Possible heart attack."

For a split second her own heart froze. Then she forced herself back into action as the patient's vital signs were read off. Nate was leaning over the man, a stethoscope magically appearing in his hand. The patient was unconscious, his breathing loud and raspy. His color didn't look good either.

They rushed him into a room. And got to work with the help of a nurse, putting leads on his chest and firing up the EKG machine.

Sasha glanced at the readout. His heart was beating but there were some telltale signs coming across the machine. "I'm seeing hyperacute *T*'s." The *T* waves were taller and more pointed than normal. It was one of the first signs of a heart attack.

"I see it. Let's get some blood readings and get some tenecteplase ready, just in case. Who's the cardiologist on call?"

The use of TNKase was still controversial in some circles, but in this case she agreed with Nate's assessment.

The nurse said, "Let me check." Two minutes later, she was back, a frown on her face. "Dr. Holloway is in emergency surgery and expected to be there for another couple of hours. I can try to call Dr. Benson at home."

"Damn." The word slid out before she could stop it. Their patient was at a critical stage. "It'll take him a half hour to get here."

Nate stripped his gloves off and pulled out his cell phone. "We're care-flighting him to The Island Clinic."

As he made the call, relief battled with irritation at the way he'd taken over. Just because he was chief of staff at The Island Clinic didn't give him the right to make decisions for Saint Victoria Hospital. But she knew he was right. Either they were going to have to treat the patient here in the ER and hope for the best, or they were going to have to rely on the specialists at the clinic, who were all top in their field. Nate had made sure of that.

She managed to grit out, "I agree."

Ha! Since he was already hanging up his phone, it hadn't really mattered what she thought. It was a done deal.

"Let's get him ready for transport."

For once she was glad for the helipad. By ambulance, the trip would have taken close to forty-five minutes, since the clinic was located on the southeast corner of the island. By helicopter it would only take seven minutes. She'd heard that magic number repeated over and over again. Another source of irritation.

They bundled everything they needed and got him to the double doors just as a low rumble signaled the chopper was headed their way. "Greg will be on that flight."

"Greg?"

"Sorry, Greg Morris. He's one of our cardiac care doctors. Since we're needed here, we won't be able to go with the patient."

"Okay." She looked at him. Really looked at him, seeing him not as just another rich man, but as a doctor who wanted what was best for his patient. *Their* patient. She put aside her negative feelings. At least for now. "Thank you. Seriously."

He nodded. Met her gaze.

"This is what I envisioned The Island Clinic being used for. To serve the island's best interests."

She hadn't really believed that, and still wasn't entirely convinced, but for the moment she was putting aside the idea that he'd only come here to cater to wealthy clientele and was using Saint Victoria Hospital as some kind of tax write-off. Maybe it was why she'd so studiously avoided him. She didn't want her suspicions to be confirmed by meeting the man. She'd be more than glad to be wrong, in this particular case.

A few seconds later, her thoughts were

only on getting the patient into the chopper and handing him off to the cardiologist on board. Then with a quick wave, the door to the helicopter closed, and they were off. She stared at it until it was out of sight then turned her gaze back to him.

"You'll let me know how he does."

His head cocked. "Sure. If you really want to know."

"Of course I do." Was he doubting that she cared about her patients? That stung. But she knew that she'd been less than welcoming toward him when they'd met.

"I could let you know…" There was a pause. "But better yet, why don't we go see him as soon as our shift here is done. If you don't have plans, that is."

She hesitated. She'd never been to The Island Clinic—had kind of made it her mission to avoid thinking about it…and Nate. But she couldn't very well tell him that. And to turn him down would seem churlish. And definitely unwelcoming. She could pretend she had a dinner engagement, but that would be yet another fib on top of her claims that she'd been in surgery so much that she'd never had a chance to meet him. She'd always prided herself on trying to do the right thing, so here was her chance to prove that. Besides, she hadn't had a date in a long, long time, something he'd easily be able to check, if he listened to the rumor mill at the hospital.

"Thanks. I'd like that."

"What time is your shift over?"

"I wasn't really scheduled today to begin with. But I'd say around five o'clock. Barring any emergencies like that last one." Hopefully there'd be no hitches and the next shift's doctors would make it in. Life at Saint Victoria Hospital could be chaotic and unpredictable, even on a good day, but she could think of nowhere she'd rather be than here at the hospital.

A call came in saying another ambulance was on its way in, so she forced her mind to return to work as she and Nate rushed back toward the ER.

Five o'clock came, and Nate realized he was exhausted. But it was a good exhaustion. He'd done his fair share of work since becoming a doctor, but over the last three years, running The Island Clinic had taken up most of his time. So he didn't often deal with emergencies like he had over the last several hours. As tired as he was, he welcomed the opportunity to get back in the thick of things. And he could see ways that the clinic had helped Saint Victoria Hospital in the glimpses of new equipment he noticed here and there. In the helipad that had whisked their heart attack patient to the facility on the other side of the island. But there was so much more to be done. So many people left to help.

If he'd given in to his parents and stayed at their facility, things would have been very different. For this hospital and for him personally. Because he'd probably be married to Tara and have a couple of kids by now.

But he hadn't stayed, and Tara had wanted no part of coming here. And it was for the best. Especially after realizing all any of them cared about was…

Stop. Just stop. He snapped his gloves off and tossed them into a nearby receptacle, just as he spotted Sasha across the space, laughing at something the male nurse next to her had said. He tensed without knowing why.

She was good at what she did. Prickly… but good. He wasn't sure why she'd been so against using his name. He'd thought maybe she held herself aloof from everyone, but no…over the day she'd called almost everyone by their given names. And every time she had, he'd tensed, seeing that flash of a smile she gave person after person. And watching the easy way she was with all of her colleagues, the way that full bottom lip formed a fake pout when someone suggested something she didn't like. Hell, his insides had shifted and quivered like some kid who was high on hormones.

And she was having a good old time talking to the man on the other side of the room…

So it was just him she didn't like. Why?

Because he was an outsider?

Maybe. He'd worked hard to fit in, but he knew at the heart of it, The Island Clinic was probably seen as a place where the wealthy came to have procedures in seclusion. And there was a lot of truth to that statement. But most of the people he'd talked to knew the main purpose of those clients was to have a steady flow of funds that would supplement Saint Victoria Hospital's shortfalls— which were sometimes huge. At those times, basic supplies could run dangerously low. Like during Hurricane Regan, which had decimated parts of the island. And his clinic wasn't just there for the wealthy. It was there for anyone who might need it. Like their heart-attack patient.

Not only that, but the clinic provided free additional training for any of the hospital's staff who might want to rotate through for a month or two. That was one of Nate's biggest sources of satisfaction. He saw it as a win-win arrangement.

He caught Sasha's eye, and like magic, her smile disappeared, that sexy lower lip straightening in what looked like disapproval as she regarded him. So maybe not everyone felt that way about The Island Clinic. If he wasn't mistaken, she didn't like him or his clinic. And he had no idea why. But she said something to the man she'd been talking to, throwing another smile and touching his arm before turning away.

His gut squeezed again. *Knock it off, Nate. It doesn't matter to you who she talks to. Who she's involved with.*

His parents had disapproved of him coming here. Had been angry that the pretty new plaque they'd made for their surgery center— the one with his name added to theirs—had had to be taken down and replaced. They'd talked about their disappointment and asked him how he could embarrass them like that. How he could disappoint Tara.

He hadn't meant to embarrass them. But he'd also never asked to be a part of their thriving practice, either. He had still had two years of his specialty training, but he'd made the decision that it wouldn't be in plastic surgery.

And when he'd told them he was using his trust fund to start The Island Clinic, they hadn't said a word, but their stony silence said it all.

They hadn't contacted Nate in the three years since he'd established the clinic. Not to see how it was doing. Not to ask how he was. And he had no idea if Tara even still worked at his parents' clinic.

To realize that those he cared about could turn their love off like some kind of spigot had done a number on him. Or maybe they hadn't wanted children at all. A thought that had plagued him for the last year. He'd had a series of nannies who had cared for him during his early childhood, since his mom had wanted to get back to work as soon as possible. When he looked at all the evidence with new eyes...

He wasn't going to think about that right now, since Sasha was now standing in front of him looking up with a frown.

Had she said something to him? "Sorry, my mind was wandering. Are you still good to go with me to the clinic?"

"I said I would."

And she kept her word, even if it was the

last thing she wanted to do. She hadn't said it outright, but the arms folded across her chest, the stiff stance said it all.

Hell, why had she agreed to come, if it was so distasteful to her? But he was too tired to challenge her or ask what was wrong. He'd done that ad infinitum with his parents and Tara after that publicity fiasco when they'd unveiled that plaque on their center less than a half hour after his flight had arrived in the States. Tara had been standing at his side and had looked at him in stunned silence when he'd shaken his head no. But no amount of explanation or sharing his heart had seemed to penetrate the united wall of ice they'd erected...the one that found them on one side and Nate firmly on the other. He'd finally given up, breaking it off with Tara and no longer trying to get through to his parents.

He wasn't anxious to expend that kind of emotional energy ever again. Especially on someone he didn't even know. If she didn't want to come, she could just say so and be done with it. "Okay, ready? We'll use the shuttle, if that's okay. Unless you'd rather use the helicopter. It'll only take a moment to call for it."

Her eyes widened, before narrowing again.

"No, I'd rather save the chopper for those who actually need it. The shuttle will be fine. Or we can use my car."

He had a feeling the less he asked of her, the better. "Let's take the shuttle, then."

Her nod had him less than sure. But again, he wasn't going to grab a shovel and try digging down to what she really meant. Because he might find that hole was a lot deeper than he had time for.

Sasha went to get her purse and to finish the last of her reports, while he went and grabbed a coffee. By the time she returned, the shuttle texted him, saying they'd arrived at the hospital.

There were three banks of seats in the back of the shuttle. He waited for her to choose one of them and then sat across the aisle from her. He wasn't going to pretend they were chummy or even friends. Because they weren't. But he damned well wasn't going to sit here in silence. He'd had enough of that to last a lifetime.

"So you've been at Saint Victoria Hospital for three years?"

She turned dark eyes on him, her lashes thicker than they had a right to be. Each blink of her eyes found his gaze tracing their path. His jaw clenched.

"Yes. Once I finished up my residency, I came back to the island."

Saint Victoria was small enough that there weren't large universities or medical schools on it. "Where did you study?"

"Harvard."

The word came fast, taking him by surprise. So much so that it took him a few seconds to process it and drum up a reply. But he didn't have time to give voice to it.

"Surprised?"

He was. But maybe not for the reasons she expected. "It's just a huge university."

"Yes, it is. And if you're wondering how I paid for it, I received a full scholarship." Her chin was tilted up as if expecting him to challenge her right to study there.

"I wasn't wondering."

Her eyes closed for a second, those lashes he'd noticed casting shadows on her cheeks. "Sorry. I'm just used to that being one of the first questions I get asked around here."

To have received a full ride at the prestigious university meant that Sasha had had top grades in all of her classes as well as on her entrance exams. He was surprised she'd chosen to come back here. She could probably practice medicine anywhere she wanted to.

Why wouldn't she come here though? He'd

chosen to, hadn't he? But he didn't care about prestige or about practicing at one of the top teaching hospitals. He just wanted to help people.

"You didn't want to stay in the States?"

She stared at him for a second before glancing away. "I thought about it for a while. But things didn't work out, so I came back home."

Didn't work out? Like at another hospital?

"Where did you do your residency?" Harvard didn't run its own hospital like Johns Hopkins did, so they partnered with other hospitals to provide places for clinicals and residencies.

"I actually did mine at Beth Israel. They place a lot of emphasis on community care, which Saint Victoria Hospital does as well, so it seemed like a good fit." She tilted her head. "Where did you study?"

"Johns Hopkins. I did my residency there, as well."

"What made you want to become a doctor?"

He was asked that on a regular basis, but it was a tricky question. He'd originally gone into premedicine because his parents had expected it of him. He'd given in mainly to explore whether it was an option for him or not.

He'd been surprised to find that he loved the classes. Loved his teachers. And loved the science of medicine.

What he didn't love was the greed that sometimes went along with it. He'd met people who went into medicine as a way to build wealth, or a reputation or to climb the social ladder. He used to think his parents had gone into medicine for altruistic reasons. And to now look at them in the cold light of day... Well, he was a little more cynical about that than he'd once been.

He decided to give the easy answer, because the true explanation was more complicated than he wanted to get into right now. "I had relatives who were doctors, so it seemed the obvious choice."

Her frown told him that what he'd said had hit a sore spot.

"So you didn't really want to be a doctor? Why be one, then?"

The tricky question became even more convoluted. "In the beginning I wasn't sure where the separation between my wants and others' expectations was. But now? Well, I can't imagine anything I'd rather be than a surgeon. And you?"

One shoulder went up. "That's easy. It was because of my dad."

She'd said it so easily. As if it didn't bother her at all. That intrigued him enough to nudge for a deeper explanation.

"Your dad?"

"He...well, he died of a heart attack when I was fourteen." Her eyes glistened with what looked like deep emotion. "There was nothing in place at that time for true emergency care. People had to be flown to a neighboring island. My dad never made it that far. He died right after arriving at a nearby clinic."

Nate shifted in his seat, reaching across to place his hand over the one she'd curled around the armrest of her chair. "I'm sorry."

The tenseness he'd been aware of in her while dealing with their patient suddenly made sense. Her need to know how he was doing. If the man had stayed at Saint Victoria Hospital, it would have been easy for her to check up on him. But at The Island Clinic, it would entail a phone call, and very probably, an explanation about why she wanted to know. No wonder she'd agreed to make the trek across the island.

Her next murmured words were soft. As if she were talking to herself. "It was a long time ago."

But not long enough to snuff the spark

of grief that appeared in her eyes when she talked about him. "Your mom?"

"She's doing fine. She's a chef, actually."

"She's still in Saint Victoria?"

"It's her home. Where else would she be?" As if she'd had second thoughts about her answer, she amended it. "This is where she was born. Where she got married. She can't imagine living anywhere else. When I thought I was going to get... Well, when I was thinking of remaining in the States, she wouldn't consider moving there. Sometimes things work out for the best, since I later decided to come back home."

Sometimes things did work out for the best. Like his deciding not to join his parents' practice? Like not caving to Tara's demands that he remain in the States? Yes. He could see now how unbearable that would have been for him. While they were perfectly happy doing what they did, Nate would have felt stifled and trapped. Maybe the estrangement was for the best. It had given him a clear road to do what he thought was right, without the constant need to run things by them, like he'd had to when he was a teenager.

It was easier this way. Right? Being alone? He realized his hand was still covering hers. He pulled away, sitting back in his seat, just as the long driveway to The Island Clinic appeared on their right.

A sliver of pride went through him when he spotted the large bronze statue out front. Marie would have approved of it, he was sure.

Glancing at Sasha, he said, "Welcome to The Island Clinic."

CHAPTER TWO

SASHA STOOD IN front of a modern white building that would rival some of the hospitals she'd seen in the States. It was on a smaller scale, but still a stunning sight on her little island. She suddenly had second thoughts about coming here.

The helipad, complete with the helicopter that had whisked their patient away, was a short distance from the building. There was a pristine asphalt driveway leading to a pair of double doors.

"*Bon Bondye*," she whispered. It was at times like this that her English failed her, the island's French Creole coming to the forefront. But it fit so much better than simply saying *Good God*.

Nate murmured something to the shuttle's driver before coming to stand beside her. "You've never been here before."

"No." What else could she say? She'd

heard it was beautiful, but that would be an understatement. It was sitting a short distance from the beach, and there was a long boardwalk that meandered from the back of the building to a white sandy shoreline, the waters calmly licking at it.

She squinted when she spotted something else. A lone figure stood down there, staring out toward the sea as if in deep thought. There were some bright umbrellas and lounge chairs scattered along the area.

Saint Victoria Hospital, on the other hand, was on the interior of Williamtown and boasted no such vistas. But then again, the staff didn't often find themselves with enough time on their hands to enjoy sights like this one.

Off to the side, there was another wing, painted in sand tones. Each of the three-story windows had a wrought iron balcony and matching table and chairs. "Is that the clinic's hotel?"

Sasha had heard it had added some accommodations that rivaled the island's own five-star Harbor Hotel.

"Yes. As you saw, the trip here from Williamtown is quite a drive. We wanted relatives to be able to stay close and for patients to be able to convalesce nearby. Would you like to see one of the rooms after we check on our patient?"

She hesitated, before saying, "Sure." It wasn't like she could just say no without sounding ungrateful for what the clinic had done for Saint Victoria Hospital. And she had to admit, she was curious about what the facility had to offer.

They went in, and Nate checked in at the desk, then came back. "They put him up in ICU. They were able to dissolve the clot and are now working to get him stable enough to put a couple of stents in."

"That's wonderful." She'd been half afraid he might have died en route. But surely Nate would have gotten a call, if that had been the case.

"Greg is really good at what he does."

She knew he didn't mean it as a criticism of the staff at Saint Victoria Hospital, but it was hard not to bristle all over again. She forced herself to breathe through it and gave him a smile. "I'm just glad that flying him over here gave him a good chance for survival."

"It did. They expect him to make a full recovery, as long as something unexpected doesn't happen. His family has arrived and will stay at the clinic's hotel while he recovers."

She didn't want to ask, but felt she had to, since she didn't want them to find themselves saddled with a huge bill. "Most of the islanders can't afford to stay in fancy hotels. Maybe I can help pay for some of it."

Nate's brown eyes cooled, like they had at Saint Victoria Hospital. "They won't be charged for staying. That's part of what we're here for."

She'd offended him. Not what she'd meant to do at all. But after her experience with Austin… Well, he never once thought about the fact that not everyone could afford the luxurious things he had. Why had she ever thought her ex could fit in with the people on Saint Victoria? Not that there weren't different socioeconomic levels here, like there were everywhere else. But only now did she realize how unequally matched they would have been.

It would be like her dating Nate.

The thought made her pause. Not that it was likely to happen. And since she'd made that mistake once before, she was now inoculated against men like him. One move in the wrong direction, and her immune system would come charging in to shut her down. Especially when it came to someone like Nate.

Although he seemed to understand the island in a way that surprised her. Warmed her. Her antibodies sat up and took notice and were readying themselves to intervene, should she do something stupid. She just hoped they arrived in time.

"I'm sorry. I just wasn't sure how it worked."

"The clinic is here for the island's hospital, not to make money off it. The patients we bring in from the outside, along with the gala, are what keep us afloat and give us the ability to help those in need."

Friends had told her time and time again that she had the wrong idea about the clinic, her friend Patty in particular, but she just hadn't been able to shake her preconceptions. Maybe it was time to start listening.

"I haven't been to one of the galas yet, but I've heard they're quite elegant."

"They are." He glanced at her. "Why don't you come to one of the planning meetings?"

"Oh, I don't know, I'm not sure you'd want my opinion."

He smiled in a way that made her stomach do a flip-flop. "I think your opinion is exactly the one we need. We actually have a meeting tomorrow night, if you're free. It's here in the conference room."

"Please don't feel like you have to invite me." The last thing she wanted was to be the token islander.

"I don't normally do things because I 'have' to. I truly do want to know what you think. Especially since you haven't been to any of the previous galas."

"I'll think about it. What time?"

"Six-thirty. We'll have dinner there, since a lot of folks will just be coming off their shift."

So the committee was made up of people working at the hospital? Not some kind of outside party-planning organization? "How many people will be there?"

"I don't know. We invite everyone." He sent her a look. "From both Saint Victoria Hospital and The Island Clinic. Whoever wants to come is welcome. You didn't know that?"

Modi. So it wasn't even just the clinic that made the decisions. "I guess I never thought about it."

"There are posters up at the hospital. I made sure of it."

Sasha had blocked out so much of the stuff about The Island Clinic that she must have chosen not to read those posters. It also made her realize that his invitation wasn't about Sasha being who she was, but about the fact that he wanted a wide range of ideas and opinions. Her knee-jerk reaction that told her to come up with an excuse not to be at that meeting fell by the wayside. "I'll try to come."

"I'll look forward to seeing you there."

They made their way up to the second-floor ICU, and Nate swiped his nametag across a keypad. The doors opened, and he waved her through. "You have to have security clearance to get in?"

He nodded. "We have everyone from high-ranking public officials to actors who come to the clinic. No one wants a picture of themselves at their most vulnerable flashed across the tabloids."

"Of course not. I didn't think about that."

The intensive-care unit was ultrahigh tech, on a scale like she'd had at Beth Israel during her residency. "What's our patient's name?"

Saying *our* gave it an intimate feeling for some reason, even though she'd used that phrase countless other times. It had to be because she'd been so resistant to meeting Nate…to working with him.

"Bill Waddel. He's in the second room on the right."

They moved toward the door, which was closed. Nate opened it and peeked in, then nodded to her that it was okay.

The man was asleep, but unlike so many who probably filled these rooms, he wasn't intubated and the number of tubes was minimal, given what he'd been through. She went to the head of the bed and noted his lips were no longer as ashen as they'd been when he was at Saint Victoria Hospital. And the heart monitor was showing a nice sinus rhythm. The *T*-waves weren't as tall or pointed. "I'd say the damage to his heart was surprisingly small, given what it could have been."

The situation could have become catastrophic if they hadn't transported him. His family might be sitting in a very different kind of room than the fancy hotel that adjoined this building.

"I agree. Greg thinks the stents he'll put in will keep the blockage from happening again. He's hoping to do the procedure tomorrow."

"That's great." The man's family wasn't here at the moment. "He's allowed to have visitors in here, isn't he?"

"Yes. His son went out to the beach to meditate, according to the front desk."

The lone figure she'd seen staring out over the water? Maybe. She looked at Nate. "Thanks for lending a hand today. The outcome might not have been the same, if you hadn't been there."

He frowned. "The hospital knows they can always refer anyone to us."

That might be so, but Sasha was ashamed to admit that she might not have been so quick to send him over. Not out of pride or arrogance, but because it simply would not have crossed her mind to call for the helicopter. But it would from now on. She didn't have to like Nate. Or The Island Clinic. But she would be negligent if she didn't take advantage of every opportunity afforded her patients. "I'll make sure to keep that in mind. Thanks for letting me see him."

He smiled again. "All you have to do is call the front desk. I want there to be collaboration between our facilities. No turf wars. Okay?"

She laughed at how well he'd read her. But maybe that wasn't such a funny thing. Hopefully he hadn't read the small jolts of attraction she'd felt from the time he showed up at Saint Victoria Hospital. Surely not. Even she hadn't been sure of what she was feeling. "Okay."

"Do you want to see the rest of the clinic?"

"I'd love to." And for once she meant it.

By the time they reached the wing with the hotel, Sasha's senses were swimming. If The Island Clinic had been here when she'd been ready for her residency, she could have probably done it here. And then stayed here to work afterward. But she'd learned a lot at Beth Israel and wouldn't trade that experience for the world. Or her time at Harvard, even if it had resulted in a broken heart and a vow to never be duped so easily again.

In reality, she hadn't been duped so much as dumped by a man who'd placed a lot less value on their relationship than she had. He was rich enough to have women standing in line to have a chance with him. She wasn't sure why she'd thought she was any more special than those others. Except the fact that she'd been young and naive of the way things worked in Austin's sphere.

He'd seemed so caring. So willing to take on the world. At least at first. But all his talk of coming to Saint Victoria had been just that. Talk.

The experience had left her cynical and

untrusting, painting everyone with the paint dipped from her ex's bucket.

Including Nate? Almost certainly, since she'd avoided him like the plague for the last three years.

"Lydia said Room 201 is vacant."

"Sorry?"

He frowned. "I was going to show you one of the rooms."

"Oh, of course."

She was being ridiculous. What had she thought he meant? That he was taking her there for reasons other than showing her around?

No, she'd learned the hard way that she was nothing special. Nate could have his choice of sleeping partners.

And given the chance, would he choose to sleep with…?

No. He wouldn't. And neither would she.

She followed him down a hallway painted in muted greens with pendant lights that were modern, but elegant. Her shoes sank into luxurious carpet, her toes curling as they wondered what it would feel like on her bare feet.

Decadent.

Just like the clinic's founder.

Even her *man*, who believed in simple

tile that was easy to clean, would be amazed at how this felt. "Do you rent rooms to tourists, as well?"

"No. The island already has a hotel that does that. I wouldn't want to take business from them. This is just for patients and their families."

"I see." She mentally ticked another box on the list of things that surprised her. "Do you have enough patients to fill this up?"

"At times. But it's not something we're aiming for. For the most part our patients have come to us as a result of word of mouth. Or if they hear about the gala and attend. We do house attendees here, if they choose to go that route. It's one of the few times we're at capacity."

"I can imagine."

They found Room 201, and Nate again used his key card to open the door. "Does that get you in anywhere you want?"

He glanced at her, that same crazy half smile curving his lips. "No. Not anywhere."

Something about the way he said that made her shiver. Her toes curled again, and this time, it had nothing to do with the carpet.

He pushed the door open and motioned her to precede him. She did and was surprised when he didn't shut the door behind them. She was grateful, though, since her thoughts had been ricocheting into some pretty questionable territory.

The room was furnished with the same deep carpeting. Two large beds, covered in what looked like down comforters, were housed in a surprisingly large space. The air conditioning was set cooler than what she was used to, but if it was true that they had A-list patients, they would probably expect no less—especially with those warm bed coverings.

He didn't say anything, so Sasha went over to the window and looked out. The room had a spectacular view of the sea and the beach. There was no sign of the man who'd been there when they'd arrived. Was he back in his hotel room with his family? Or were they with Bill?

She didn't even know if that was the same man Nate had been referring to.

"This is gorgeous."

"Yes. I agree."

His voice was a little closer than it had been. And for a second time, she was glad that door had been left open. Not because she was afraid he might try something, but because she was afraid she might lose sight of what lay outside that room. Because in here, everything felt magical. Unreal. As if fairy tales might actually exist in real life.

She'd thought that once before. But it had turned out to be a lie.

"Sometimes you don't realize how things look to people who aren't from here. But this view… It's like something out of a magazine."

"Saint Victoria is beautiful. It's easy to become blind to the beauty around us, when we see it day after day."

"Yes. It is." She glanced back to see him watching her. "Is it okay if I go out onto the balcony?"

"Yes. Of course."

She unlocked the door with fingers that were shaking slightly. Because of him? Or the view? Maybe a little of both.

The balmy sea breeze slid over her face, beckoning her closer. Going over to the rail, she laid her arms on the black ironwork. The scent of salt and all that lived in the water was intoxicating. She leaned her head back and breathed deeply. She could only imagine the battle between worry and being bewitched by this locale families might experience. Maybe even Bill's son. This would be the perfect place to meditate. To relish being alive. Nate came beside her and leaned a hip on the railing as he turned to look at her. "It's a nice spot, isn't it?"

"I think nice might be the understatement of the year. It's amazing. I'm so glad The Island Clinic was able to build here."

She was surprised to find it was the truth.

"Really? I got the feeling you weren't all that thrilled with us being here."

"Dr. Edwards, I just—"

"Nate. Please."

The way he said it, made her heart twist. She really was being unreasonable about it. And in her attempt to maintain her distance, she could see that she'd probably come off as ridiculous.

"Okay. Nate…" Except saying his given name…out loud…made whatever she'd been about to say vanish. So she just stood there, taking in his casual clothing that was now rumpled in a way that was somehow wonderful. The hard lines of his body were more visible now, and she was having a difficult time looking away. Her gaze trailed up his face, noting there were dark circles under his eyes, probably from the stress of the day. She imagined he put in long hours most every day. A little far removed from the lap-of-luxury living she'd pictured him in over in this corner of the island.

"Not so hard, after all, was it?"

"W-what?" Had he read her thoughts?

"Saying my name."

Her senses went on high alert as an image of her whispering his name in an entirely different way scurried through her head, only to run away when she tried to catch it and banish it. Instead, the two beds in the room behind her seemed to taunt her, to remind her of how long it had been since she'd been with anyone.

She cleared her throat. "Maybe I was being a little silly when we met. I'd just heard stories…"

"Stories?" His frown was back. "Such as?"

Um, not happening. Because the words *delectable* and *delicious* had been interjected time and time again. "Nothing bad."

That line in his face played peekaboo. "I find that rather hard to believe."

"That nothing bad was said?"

He made a sound of assent. "Are you saying *you've* never had an unkind thing to say about me?"

Ugh. She'd had lots of unkind things to

say. Patty had called her on it numerous times. But then again, her friend was a newlywed, still caught up in the early stages of love.

Her lips twitched. "Maybe you'll have to work on changing my mind."

"Is that a challenge… Sasha?"

The shock of hearing her name on his tongue washed over her like the waves of the sea. Warm. Sensual. Snaking up her calves, edging over her hips and making her nipples tighten.

Some dangerous part of her brain sent the word "Maybe" from her mouth before she could stop it.

And when his hand moved from the railing and slid up her forearm, she was powerless to stop from leaning toward him, her eyes closing.

"That's one challenge I might have to accept." The low words made the sensuous fog that was slowly enveloping her body thicken.

Kiss me!

Thank God she hadn't said the words aloud, but she'd definitely sent them out into the stratosphere. But his mouth didn't cover hers. After several agonizing seconds, she opened her eyes.

She found him staring at her, a muscle working in his jaw. Then he let go of her arm. "I'm sure you're tired, especially since this was supposed to be your day off."

"I—I…" Her mind scrambled for something witty to say. Something that didn't make her look as much of a fool as she felt. "I am. I should probably head home."

"You'll still come to the meeting?"

That was about the worst thing she could think of at the moment. Her reaction to him had been electric. Crazy. She'd been so sure he was going to kiss her.

But obviously that hadn't been on his mind. Or if it had, he'd thought better of it.

Smart on his part.

She took a step backward, only to find herself trapped by the metal portion of the balcony. Instead, Nate moved away, motioning for her to go through the doors where those two big beds sat. Beds that she'd seen herself writhing on moments earlier.

God. How stupid was she?

Hadn't she already fallen into that trap once before, of falling in love with someone with power and money?

Well, she wasn't going to do that again. From now on, her heart was going to be on guard against Nate's good looks. Against his low voice, against that seductive dimple in his cheek.

And most of all. She was going to be on guard against herself.

CHAPTER THREE

"But why do you need to bring in an outside catering service? Why not use something from here on the island?"

Sasha could feel everyone's eyes on her the moment she spoke. She'd vowed to herself that she'd not say anything, especially since misreading his signals last night had made it hard to sleep. Hard to even contemplate attending tonight.

For the most part, she'd sat quietly. But she couldn't stop herself from asking the question.

Nate moved back to the podium, his eyes meeting hers. Something flashed in his gaze, and she wasn't sure if it was curiosity or irritation. "Okay, tell me what you would do."

"I would hire local DJs or musicians, contract food and services from here, play up what we have to offer. If you're hoping to bring in outside contributions, then you make this personal—memorable—rather than just another of a hundred fund-raisers that they've attended in the past."

His face remained passive, and she floundered a bit, wondering if maybe she was wrong. Nate had been doing this just fine, without her help for the last three years. And if what she'd seen of the clinic was anything to go by, then he'd been successful beyond anyone's wildest dreams. But he'd wanted her input, right? Had asked her to come. The least she could do was give him what he was asking for.

"And you know of a company here on the island that can provide services on a large scale? We're hoping to host between eight hundred to a thousand guests. I'd asked around before and from what I understood, there isn't a catering service that does events of this size."

She swallowed. Okay, so maybe she didn't know what she was talking about. And he was probably right about there not being a catering company that specialized in massive events. But surely it was just a matter of multiplying people, resources, waitstaff, etc. If what Nate said was true, and he was doing all of this for Saint Victoria, surely the folks here would want to be involved in that.

It wasn't just a matter of having a telethon or television spot and expecting people to start pulling out their checkbooks. This should be a partnership between those on the island and those from the outside who wanted to help.

Nate shouldn't be carrying this on his own.

"Have you already contracted with an outside catering company?"

"We've had bids from several places. Tonight we were going to choose one of them."

So maybe it was too late. Maybe this was something that should be talked about for next year, not this one. But, her mom was one of the best organizers around and a super cook. If she asked her to round up people to cook and decorate, she had no doubt that Tessi James could get it done. She already made cakes for local weddings and food for several restaurants. If you got five or ten people like her, they could easily cover that kind of project. And if Nate rejected her idea outright? Well then, her opinion of him would drop back to what it had originally been: a rich man who had the money to throw at things, like caterers and fancy accoutrements, but didn't want to actually roll his sleeves up and work alongside everyone else.

And maybe she could get her weird attraction to him back under control.

Except he'd worked beside her at Saint Victoria Hospital to save Bill Waddel's life.

That gave her the courage to speak up yet again. "What if we could pull together a team from here on the island to do that? The caterers are going to decorate, as well?"

"Yes. They would bring in all of their own equipment and china."

China. Okay, so she hadn't thought about that. Enough for eight hundred to a thousand people?

She licked her lips. "Would it be possible to put off making the decision for a couple more days? I know someone who I think could organize something on this scale."

Nate crossed his arms over his chest. "You do? Can I have a name?"

Okay, it was now or never. And he certainly had a right to know. She only hoped he didn't see this as her wanting to throw business her mother's way. In actuality, she needed to ask her mom before she committed her to something, which was why she'd asked for a couple of days. "Tessi James."

Murmurs went up around the room, and she glanced around to see nods and smiles from some of the folks from Saint Victoria Hospital. Many of them knew her mother from catering their own baby showers, weddings and family celebrations.

Nate's eyes were scanning the room, as well. "I see some of you know who this person is and…" His gaze swung back to her. "Tessi James. Would she happen to be any relation to you, Dr. *James*?"

Oh, this was exactly what she'd been afraid of. "Yes, she's my mom. But…" She turned to those in attendance. "How many of you have used my mom for your events?"

Hands lifted from all over the group. Probably twenty people.

"I see." Nate addressed Sasha again. "And you think she could pull off a formal event for this many people?"

He uncrossed his arms, his hands dropping to land on hips that were far too lean for comfort. Hips she'd imagined moving over hers on one of those hotel beds. His fingers tightened and her mouth went dry as shocking scenes of those hands closing on her flesh strobed through her head in snatches that were erotic beyond belief. She lost her train of thought for several scary seconds.

Clearing her throat, she managed to find her voice again. "It…um…depends what you mean by formal. If you're talking formal by Saint Victoria standards, then yes. But that might not look like what you're used to." She heaved a breath and forced her eyes back to his face. "I would venture to say, however, that it will be memorable and special…and it won't embarrass you."

Nate's brows went up. "That never even crossed my mind. I was merely talking numbers, not whether or not your mother was capable of hosting an event."

"Which is why I'd like a day or two to talk to her. To talk to you, to see what you've done in the past and what you're hoping to accomplish at this year's event."

Was she crazy? She actually wanted to meet with him…alone? After last night? After the thoughts she'd just had about him?

And by committing her mom to having a part in the planning process, she'd committed herself to meeting with him on more occasions. So much for guarding her heart.

"Okay, let's put it to a vote. If you would like to explore keeping the catering local, raise your hands."

Every hand in the room went up, even people she didn't recognize, who probably worked here at The Island Clinic, most of whom had been brought in from other countries.

Her chest tightened, and her attitude took another slight shift.

"It seems it's unanimous. I'll give you three days to explore this avenue. But I'd like to meet with you after we're done here to discuss the particulars, okay?"

The way he said that made her shiver. She wasn't sure if he was angry or amenable to her suggestion. But she guessed she would find out soon enough.

Nate had been at Saint Victoria Hospital again today, so he had to be exhausted. She hadn't worked with him, this time, but she had caught glimpses of him every so often. She'd been relieved to be away from him. That encounter in the hotel room had been...

Fabulously sexy. If they'd actually kissed, maybe she could have put it behind her and moved on. As it was, she was picturing him doing a lot more than just kissing her.

But she knew how easily things could go from fabulous to horrifying, so she was better off not having any of those thoughts come to fruition.

He was waiting for her response. So she said the only thing she could think of. "Yes, of course."

While the meeting continued, revolving around timing and guest accommodations, she sent a quick text to her mom.

Hey, how do you feel about getting a catering crew together to serve one thousand people? Formal, islander style.

There was a pause, then her phone vibrated.

When?

Ha! Her mom had not batted an eye. Just like Sasha had suspected. Her fingers moved over the phone's keypad.

About a month away.

Let me check with some people and look at my calendar, but I think it's doable. When do you need an answer?

After Sasha's dad died, her mom had thrown herself into her little business, and had made a name for herself in terms of catering and party planning and cake decorating.

In just a couple of days. It's for The Island Clinic's yearly gala.

I'll get right on it and have an answer by Monday, if you can get me the details.

Whew. Sasha had wondered if she'd opened her big mouth before engaging her brain...which she had, but her mom was covering her back. I'll text you when I get home and can come by the house tomorrow, if that's okay.

She had the day off, although if the hospital got too busy, she was willing to work through it. There was no word yet on when Dr. Warren would be back to work. Hopefully his family member was doing better.

See you then. Mwen renmen ou.

Love you too, Mom!

The meeting dismissed soon afterward, with people going their separate ways. Patty Cohen sidled up to her. "Good idea suggesting your mom head up the catering. Will she do it, do you think?"

Sasha laughed. "I was being bad and texting her during part of the meeting. If her calendar is clear, and she can get enough help, I think she'll agree to do it."

"That's really great. And I'm glad you decided to come to the meeting, for once." The exasperated face Patty made was totally fake. Her friend had been trying to coax her to be more involved with things that went on at The Island Clinic for quite a while and hadn't understood why Sasha was so resistant to the idea. Or why she'd taken a dislike to its chief of staff.

Well, even Sasha couldn't understand it. It probably had something to do with Austin and the pain he'd inflicted on her. Five years of dating, and just when she'd been expecting a marriage proposal, she'd gotten a breakup text instead, saying he'd decided to go on staff at a large New York hospital.

He'd had the audacity to conclude with an invitation for her to *drop by*, if she were ever in New York. They could get together for drinks. She was pretty sure she knew what the invitation entailed: sex with no strings attached. So much for his talk of coming to Saint Victoria to work.

It was the first time she'd realized how big a rift there was between her and some of her wealthier classmates. And it had been just in time for her to leave for Beth Israel. Everything about her experience at Harvard had been tainted by what Austin had done.

It had probably also tainted her view of Nate and his clinic.

"I'm glad I came too."

Patty took a step back. "Looks like you're

being paged, and Dax is waiting for me at home, so I'm going to head out. We need to have lunch. It feels like we haven't gotten together in ages."

Her friend's whirlwind romance with an old flame had been the talk of Saint Victoria Hospital. But from the look of it, her friend was deliriously happy. And she was genuinely glad for them both.

She glanced to the side to see that Nate was standing a short distance away, waiting for her.

"It's been busy with Marcus gone. Hopefully he'll be back soon. But yes, let's plan lunch once my schedule clears out a bit." She gave Patty a quick hug and then said goodbye, moving toward Nate.

She threw him an apologetic look. "I hope I didn't mess anything up with my suggestion. And really, I probably had no right to make it, since I haven't been to any of the other meetings. Or any of the galas."

"It's why I asked you to come. I did see you texting during the last part of it."

So he had noticed. "Sorry, I was texting my mom. If there wasn't any possibility she could do it, I was going to withdraw the idea."

"I thought that might be it. It was a good

idea, and I'm not sure why I didn't check any further when I was told there wasn't a caterer large enough to handle it."

Because he knew one way of doing things, and it was hard to think of what you didn't know. She was pretty sure it really had been just an oversight, rather than a snub. "What you don't know, you don't know."

"Thanks for that. I never want to seem like a bulldozer coming in and running over people." He tilted his head. "And I somehow get the idea that's what you've thought of me."

Time to tread lightly. "Maybe. I'm hoping I was wrong about you."

His mouth quirked. "I'm hoping you were wrong too." He glanced at the phone in her hand. "So what did she say? Your mom, I mean?"

"She's going to check with some folks and said she'd have an answer to me by Monday."

"Good. I set another meeting for Tuesday. Can you have some ideas back to me before then?"

"How about if I bring her in to meet with you that morning, if she's free?"

He nodded. "She can do it that quickly?"

Sasha laughed. "You might not be a bulldozer, but my mom has been known to flatten anyone who gets in her way."

"In that case, remind me never to stand in her path. Seriously, though, it won't leave her much time to get a menu and plans in place. Can she do the cutlery and so forth?"

"I think so. I'll need to know exactly what she needs, if you have time to give me a run-down."

"Yes, let's go back to my office. Most of the paperwork is in there, and they need to clean the conference room."

Sasha turned and noted there were people already stacking chairs and picking up dis-carded coffee cups. "Oh, of course."

A frisson of excitement went through her as she followed Nate down the hallway. She hoped it was due to the idea of helping plan a small part of the gala, but she was pretty sure most of it had to do with the man him-self. She'd dreamed about that almost kiss last night. Except it hadn't stopped at a kiss. It had turned hot and wet and wicked. Her face heated and she was glad, very glad, he wasn't looking at her right now.

At the very end of the hallway, Nate used his key card to open a door on the right and stood back to let her move past him. She walked in, and frowned, all thoughts of her dream disappearing. His office was huge, with a long leather sofa and seating area off to the left, and a heavy wooden desk and matching leather chairs to the right.

The carpet was the same thick pile as what she'd seen in the hotel and cushioned her every step. Thank God, because her feet were killing her.

He must have noticed her reaction, because he moved around to grab some file folders from the desk and motioned her toward the seating area. "I meet with people in here all the time."

She could imagine he did. How better to coax checkbooks to open than to meet them in a place where things looked like they did in their own fancy offices.

But it also was a reminder of how different they were. Of how alike he and Austin were. Both presented themselves as wealthy philanthropists. Austin's was just a thin, shiny layer that didn't go more than skin deep. And Nate's? Well, the jury was still out on that.

The bottom line was, she and Nate were from two different worlds, and she'd better stop dreaming about the man before she did something stupid. Or got hurt all over again. So she paid careful attention to the things in the room. Custom artwork that looked to be done by local artisans decorated the walls. On a set of shelves behind the sofa were colorful bottles that probably contained various types of liquor.

As if reading her thoughts, he said, "Would you like something to drink?"

Suddenly she did. And since she'd come to the clinic via the shuttle, she'd be taking it back home again, which meant she wouldn't have to drive. It also made her realize the vehicle would probably be making that trip just for her. "I hate to ask the shuttle to come back—"

"I'll take you back to the hospital. Or you can stay in one of the guest rooms here."

Like in Room 201? The one he'd shown her yesterday? No. She wouldn't be doing that. "I'd appreciate the ride, if that's okay."

"I am the one who asked you to stay after class, so it's the least I can do."

That made her smile. "I was the one who volunteered up my mom. But thank you. And I'd like a glass of red wine, if you have it." It had been a long day, and she could use something to help her unwind a bit.

"I do." He went over to the seating area and reached into a small glass-fronted refrigerator. Ah, a wine cooler.

While he retrieved a footed glass and a tumbler and fixed their drinks, she walked around the office. Her big toe twinged as it hit the end of her shoe. These were coming off as soon as she got home.

Something on a shelf behind his desk caught her eye. Something that didn't match the rest of the sumptuous surroundings. The discomfort in her feet disappeared as she moved closer.

A small cloth doll sat on top of a book that had been tipped on its side. Its hair was cut from pieces of brown yarn and stuck up in all directions, and the undyed muslin of the body and dress were simple. It looked like a doll that some of the moms on the island fashioned for their daughters. She couldn't picture him buying something like this.

She studied it. The facial features were embroidered, and the black shoes were stitched from felt. There were smudges of what looked like dirt here and there and the thread on one of the shoes was fraying. Her eyes widened. This doll had been played with, not purchased from one of the island's tourist shops.

She realized that the clinking of glassware had stopped and when she looked at Nate, she saw he was watching her with a glass of amber liquid in his hand. He took a sip of it. Then another.

"This is an interesting doll. Did you know

that mothers here sometimes make these for their daughters? I had one when I was younger. I probably still have it somewhere, in fact."

"Yes. I knew." He took another sip of his drink and came over to her with the glass of wine. His eyes were not on the doll. They were on something off to the side.

Her curiosity got the best of her. "Where did you get it?"

A muscle worked in his cheek, looking much like it had last night. A sense of foreboding came over her, and Sasha thought for a minute he wasn't going to answer her question. Then he said, "It was given to me. Let's go talk about the gala, shall we?" His hand gestured toward the sofa on the other side of the room.

He'd made it about as plain as it could be. He didn't want to talk about the doll. But why? Well, that was his prerogative, and this time, she wasn't going to butt in where she wasn't welcome. With one last glance at the lonely figure on the shelf, she took her wine and walked back over to the couch.

People had asked Nate about Marie's doll before, and he'd always responded to them without hesitation. But when he'd noticed

Sasha studying it, a rock had suddenly gathered in the pit of his stomach. It was the last thing he'd wanted to talk about after the meeting about a glitzy fund-raising gala, even though a portion of the money would go toward awareness of schistosomiasis, including water testing and prevention, as well as antibody tests and treatment.

So he'd snatched at the excuse to talk about something else. Anything else. But the second Sasha's face had closed in on itself, he knew he'd been blunt. Too blunt. But unless he wanted to go into a full-scale explanation, it was too late to rectify his mistake.

She sat on the couch, stiff and unyielding, and held her phone tightly in her hands. "So tell me about the meals you've had in the past."

He hesitated, the need to confide in her sneaking up on him again. He shook his head to rid himself of the impulse. Sitting in the chair across from her, he opened one of the file folders he'd brought over. In it were pictures from the past three galas. All three of them very different, but each of them elegant in its own way.

"These are shots from our other events. It doesn't have to look exactly like these though."

Sasha took the pictures from him and studied them, turning some of them sideways when the perspective changed. A movement caught his eye. She was methodically raising the heel of her right foot in and out of her shoe. She lifted it for a second or two before wiggling it back down. Up again, then pushing it back down.

Her feet hurt. She'd probably been in those shoes all day, and now he'd asked her to stay in them even longer. Well, technically she'd asked to speak with him, but still...

"Sasha." He waited for her to look up before he finished. Her dark eyes met his, a question in their depths. "You can take your shoes off, if you'd like. Your feet look like they're bothering you."

Her nose squinched up in a way that made his stomach twist. "I was trying to be subtle, but yes, they're new and it was stupid of me to have worn them today."

"No one will see you in here." He smiled. "It will be our little secret."

She blinked, eyes holding his. "Are you sure?"

"Sure that it will be a secret?" He nodded at the sheaf in her hands. "I promise it won't end up in that file folder."

Sasha laughed and the sound tickled something in his chest, and he let the weight of Marie and that doll slide away. At least for a few minutes.

"Okay, then, as long as you promise."

"I do."

She slid her feet from the shoes, using one to push the footwear to the side. Then she let them sink into the carpet, her toes actually curling into it and tightening on the fibers. Parts down low tightened, flickered to life.

Damn. Time to talk about something else.

Before he could, though, Sasha sighed. "Thank you. This feels heavenly."

Yes, it did. And it had nothing to do with the carpet. "I've been known to stretch out on it, when my back is hurting."

Her brows went up. "You have back problems?"

"Just the normal twinges from age." He'd fallen from a swing set as a child and every once in a while his L2 vertebra ached.

"Age…righ-h-ht."

The way she drew the word out forced a laugh from him. "It's either blame age or stupidity for it."

"Stupidity?"

"Let's just say jumping from a swing into a mud puddle doesn't always go as planned.

It's all in the landing. And this one wasn't good."

"Ouch." Her head tilted. "I can't picture you swinging."

For some reason the last word caught his attention in a totally inappropriate way. A funny retort came to mind, only she might not find it nearly as funny. "For good reason. The only place I swing nowadays is on my hammock."

"Hammock? You have one?"

"I do. The catering team actually borrowed it for one of the galas. There should be a picture in there somewhere."

He moved to the couch, anxious to shift his thoughts in another direction. She handed him the snapshots and he sifted through them, finding the one he was looking for. "Here."

Sasha leaned closer to look at it to study the scene. Rough wooden pillars that were made to look like tree trunks boasted snaking vines and twinkle lights. His hammock was strung between two of them, layered with pillows and some kind of throw blanket.

"I love that. Something like this would be very doable for my mom. It wouldn't look exactly like this, obviously, but a tropical theme would really fit with Saint Victoria."

"Yes, I think this was my favorite gala."

"I can see why."

Her toes shifted in the carpet yet again, sending a sudden shaft of heat through his midsection. Her toenails were bare of polish and looked clean and natural. She was completely different from Tara. But then again, his former girlfriend had to maintain a polished appearance for his parents' clinic.

Not that Sasha lacked polished. She just didn't need it. There was a beauty about her that…

He cleared his throat. "So you think your mom can do this?"

"I don't *think* she can. I know she can. She's amazing."

Her mom wasn't the only one who was amazing.

Sasha's eyes came up, and he realized he hadn't responded to her statement. But right now, he wasn't sure he could come up with anything coherent. "Are you worried, Nate?"

He was. But it had nothing to do with the gala and everything to do with her. And the crazy jolt he always got when she said his name. Maybe it was because she'd made such a big deal about not using it. But, more likely, it was the way her velvety tones wrapped around the sounds, holding on to them before releasing them into the air.

"No." He paused. "Are you?"

Her thumb brushed across the glossy surface of one of the prints. "I…wasn't."

"Until now?"

She nodded, the tip of her tongue coming out to moisten her lips. That's when he knew. She felt the change in atmosphere, just like he had. It was the same sensation he'd gotten on the balcony last night.

Maybe it would keep happening every time they were in a room together. Unless he did something radical about it. Something to quench the sparks that were starting to sting the lining of his chest.

Maybe one kiss would put it behind him, just like it had with any other woman he'd been with since he'd broken things off with Tara.

Or maybe it would be like that accident on the swing, where what he'd thought would happen when he jumped ended up turning into something he'd never do again.

Wasn't that the same thing? Either way, he'd try it once and be done with it.

He set down the picture he was still holding in his hand, and took the ones she had. Then he stood to his feet, reaching for her hand.

When she placed her fingers on his palm, it was as if an electric current surged through him, holding him fast in its grip. It was there when he closed his fingers around hers. It was there when he slowly pulled her to her feet.

And it was still there when his palms cupped her face, his thumbs sliding over it in a way that mimicked what she'd done with the photo a few minutes ago.

Suddenly he realized this was nothing like jumping from a swing and misjudging his landing. This was going to be far more dangerous. But like that foolish decision to leap out into the air, it was already too late to reconnect with the swing. All he could do was sail into space, and hope he survived the fall.

CHAPTER FOUR

HIS FACE WAS inches from hers. But he wasn't moving any closer. Not so his fingers, which were brushing across her skin in a way that drove her wild.

Please, please don't pull away this time.

The second his gaze landed on her, she shuddered. The molten depths of his pupils said this was nothing like last time.

"I just needed to see," he muttered. "Just needed to know…"

Then his mouth was on hers, and her world turned inside out.

She wasn't sure how this had happened. One moment they'd been talking about the gala. But when he'd come to sit next to her, her heart had started drumming in her chest as fear and anticipation swirled to life inside her. Fear that this was going to end up like last night. But anticipation that it might not. Maybe this time…

And it was better than even her sexiest dream. His mouth was plastered to hers as if he couldn't get enough. And the feel of it was shattering and amazing all at once.

His hand sank into her hair, his fingers closing around it. But it wasn't to control. It was as if he needed to anchor himself somehow. And she relished it, relished the reality of his arms around her.

His lips left her mouth, trailing to her ear, nipping at the lobe and making her shiver.

"Nate…" The whispered word came out before she could stop it. But he'd talked about lying on the floor, and right now, the carpeting seemed so inviting. How easy would it be to just sink down and have him follow her. Cover her body with his…

Images flooded her mind, causing parts of her to soften in readiness.

Or there was the couch.

Her hand went to the back of his head, drawing him back to her mouth. She opened, and his tongue accepted her silent invitation, sliding in and filling her, making her whimper with need.

A sudden loud knock at the door shocked her into immobility. Then she realized what it was and wheeled backward, their mouths coming apart, hand in her hair sliding free.

The back of her hand went to her mouth, trying to yank her brain back from wherever she'd left it.

His eyes speared hers. "Hell, sorry, Sasha. I…"

"Answer it."

The reality was, if he said anything to her right now, she was likely to burst into tears.

Giving her one last glance, he strode over to his desk, standing behind it before he told whoever it was to come in.

The door opened and a face she didn't recognize glanced her way for a second before looking back at Nate.

"We have a chopper coming in bringing a patient who has severe injuries to his arm and leg after being pulled into a piece of machinery. The leg was almost severed…he's lost a lot of blood and right now and Dr. Sizer is on vacation, so—"

"I'm on my way. Get him as stable as you can and grab an operating room."

"Thanks."

The man withdrew.

"Sorry, Sasha, I need to—"

"I'm coming with you. I'm a surgeon and you might need some help." The temptation to just fade away into the night was strong, but she wasn't going to leave a patient in need. Besides, Nate was her ride home.

And that kiss? Not something she was going to think about right now.

He hesitated for a minute before nodding and saying, "Thank you."

It was then that she realized that her feet were still bare and her shoes were somewhere behind her. God! Hopefully the man at the door had been too busy to notice, or too concerned about the patient to care.

And right now, that's exactly what she needed to be. Too concerned to care.

Nate glanced at Sasha as she stuffed her feet back into her shoes, remembering they were hurting her. But he really did need the help. Grant Sizer was their trauma surgeon and this was his field. But Nate had dealt with some pretty traumatic injuries.

They went down in the elevator and out onto the surgical floor.

"Operating room three," one of the nurses called out as they hurried by.

Side by side they scrubbed in at adjoining sinks. Side by side they entered the room and allowed two surgical nurses to glove them up.

Nate went over to the table and took over

from the ER doctor who had been overseeing the process of keeping the man alive.

"What have we got?"

"Severe spiral lacerations to the right arm, and the right leg is basically held together by the bone. Much of the soft tissue has been sliced all the way through. We've clamped the arteries." He looked at him. "We're going to need several hands on deck for this one."

He glanced at the IV pole next to the man's head, where a pint of blood was already hung and dripping.

"Dr. James is a surgeon from Saint Victoria Hospital. If you can find me a microsurgeon, we'll tag team it."

"I've got one on call now."

"Good." He glanced at Sasha. "Can you take a look at the arm, while I tackle the leg?"

"Of course."

"We'll need a couple of sets of instruments."

One of the nurses stepped forward. "We're ready for you. We have other surgical nurses on standby if needed."

His hospital had always run like clockwork and this was one of those times that he was extremely grateful it did.

He moved to the patient's leg and assessed

the injuries. It was bad. And just like the other doctor had said. There were huge slashes in the midthigh through which pearly bone was visible. The bone had probably prevented the limb from being completely severed. He could handle reattaching the large swaths of muscle and skin, if they could get the microsurgeon to work on the smaller vessels and nerves.

"How are you up there?"

Sasha glanced up at him, her eyes sharp and aware. Thank God they'd barely had any alcohol. That kiss had interrupted all of that. Strange that he should be grateful for something that never should have happened, but he was.

"Several deep cuts, but they haven't reached the bone. Lots of work to piece everything back together, but I can do it."

Thank God she'd stayed. "Thanks, Sasha. Go ahead and start."

She nodded at him, her eyes crinkling above her mask as she smiled. "I already have."

It was then that he noticed the needle and suture material in her hand.

Time passed in a way that was surreal whenever he was in surgery. It both dragged and sped by as he sutured by rote. The microsurgeon had arrived within fifteen minutes of being called and they both worked on different sections with the other surgeon doing the finer work and Nate doing the bulkier repairs. Periodically he glanced up at Sasha and saw her eyes fixed on what she was doing, the concentration on her face intense as she worked silently, calling out for different instruments periodically.

As he put the last suture in place, he glanced up at the clock and saw six hours had gone by.

And Sasha was nowhere to be seen. The arm was neatly bandaged, so she'd finished it all by herself.

They woke the patient up, and thankfully he regained consciousness fairly quickly. After losing almost half of his blood volume, there'd been the fear of brain damage. But he responded to simple questions with a nod. Then he was wheeled away into recovery.

Ted Daly, the microsurgeon, clapped him on the back. "Good work. I think we saved his leg. I didn't even see his arm. How bad was it?"

"Not nearly as bad as what we had, from what Dr. James said."

Ted glanced his way. "Did she already leave?"

"I'm not sure. She's from Saint Victoria

Hospital, came here for the meeting on the gala."

"Right. I thought I recognized her. I liked her ideas of using local businesses."

"Yes, so did I." He mused, glad that everyone seemed positive about those suggestions. But right now, he was wondering where she'd gone. Had she asked for the shuttle to come after all?

He didn't want her to leave without trying to figure out what had happened between them in his office. Or at least figure out where to go from here. How to backtrack and not let this interfere with their working relationship, since with her mom's involvement in the gala there was bound to be some overlap.

"Well, I'm headed home again. If you see Dr. James before I do, please thank her. She probably saved us a couple more hours of work tonight."

If he saw her before Ted did? Was the man going to seek her out?

And if he did? It should mean nothing to him. Nothing at all.

"I will. See you tomorrow."

Ted's brows went up. "I think you mean today."

The man was right. It was almost four in

the morning. "Right. Go home and try to get some sleep."

"You, as well. See you."

With that, they parted ways, both stripping off their PPE and heading out the doors.

Nate turned toward the nurses' desk to ask if they'd seen Sasha, passing the waiting room as he did. He glanced over there just as he went by, then backtracked when he saw a familiar profile. She had her arm draped over the back of the chair next to her and her head rested in the crook of her elbow. He thought at first she was asleep, but she lifted her head and looked at him.

"How is he?"

"He woke up. Seems conscious. We won't know fully about his leg for a couple of days, but it pinkened up once the blood flow was restored to it."

"That's good. I wondered."

"Ted asked me to thank you. I'll add my thanks to his. The repairs to his arm went okay?"

"Yes. The damage looked worse than it actually was once I started working."

Her feet were out of her shoes again.

"How are they?"

She looked up at him. "Sorry?"

"Your feet. They were hurting before, and

that was before you stood on them for six more hours."

"They'll survive." Her teeth came down on her lower lip. "I hate to ask, but would it be okay if I stayed in the hotel? The thought of getting up and walking on them again isn't thrilling, and I hate to ask you to drive forty-five minutes one way."

"Of course. Do you have to be at the hospital this morning?"

"No, not until the afternoon."

"Okay, let's get you checked in and you can get some sleep. And I'll take you home sometime after lunch."

She sighed. "Thank you."

"No, Sasha. Thank you. We'll discuss the other...stuff after we've both gotten some rest."

Her glance met his before skipping away. "I appreciate that."

She put her shoes on yet again, wincing this time as she did so before getting to her feet. "I'm ready. Can I just ask one thing?"

"Sure."

"Can you ask for a room other than 201?"

Room 201? Oh, hell, it was where they'd stood on the balcony. The first time he realized he wanted to kiss her. That time he'd been able to take a step back.

He wasn't going to acknowledge he knew what she was talking about though. Instead, he simply said, "Sure. That won't be a problem."

Then without another word he turned and led the way to the elevator, which would take them to the ground floor. And the hotel.

CHAPTER FIVE

HE WAS SUPPOSED to meet with Tessi James and Sasha today and talk about the possibility of catering it locally. He glanced at the shelf where Marie's doll was and was tempted to take it down and stuff it in a drawer. It was probably what had led to that ill-fated kiss. Something that never should have happened. But to do so felt sacrilegious, almost—as if protecting his own comfort was more important than the reality of what had happened to that little girl.

And why hadn't he shared its meaning with Sasha? Maybe it was just embarrassment that he hadn't been able to recognize what was wrong with the child. But it truly had been too late, even if he'd figured it out. Her liver had failed and there was no bringing her back from it.

So he left the doll where it was, and waited for the knock on his door that would signal Tessi's arrival. Five minutes after the appointed meeting time, he glanced at his phone with a frown. They were late. Had Tessi decided it was too big a project to take on? Had Sasha told her what had happened between them and talked her into backing out? Hell, why hadn't he talked to her about what had happened?

Because he hadn't had the chance. She'd disappeared before he'd even gotten back to the hospital. The hotel said she'd left at nine that morning, taking the shuttle back on one of its regularly scheduled trips.

So maybe neither Tessi nor Sasha was coming. Thankfully, he hadn't yet responded to any of the prospective caterers from the States.

As he was looking at his text messages, the phone in his hand rang, and he almost dropped the thing.

Dammit! What is wrong with you? Shaking his head and sighing, he pressed the button to answer. "Nate Edwards here."

"I'm sorry, Dr. Edwards, but I think your appointment is here."

"Good. Send them up, please."

"Um…there are like twenty people here. Do you want them all in your office?"

He blinked. Glanced at his office. He could hold ten people easily in here, but twenty? He had no idea anyone other than Tessi and Sasha were coming. "Can you direct them to the conference room at the hotel, if nothing is scheduled there?"

A few seconds went by. "I don't see anything. Okay, I'll send them over."

Marie's doll wouldn't be an issue after all. Nor would meeting Sasha in a place he'd made such a huge mistake. He had never kissed a colleague here or anywhere else. And he was going to make sure his little lapse of judgement never happened again. Still, he couldn't help but ask. "Is Sasha James with them?"

"I'm not sure who that is—"

"It's okay—I'll just meet them over there."

After shutting the door to his office, he made his way over to the hotel wing and sure enough, there was a small crowd of people walking in that direction. And Sasha *was* with them. A weird sense of relief washed over him.

He unlocked the door and let them through, wrapping his fingers around Sasha's wrist to hold her back for a second. He realized that was a mistake when his fingers tingled from the contact. Hell, he'd thought the kiss might somehow satisfy whatever strange curiosity he'd had toward her. Evidently that wasn't so.

He forced out, "What's going on?"

"I'm as surprised as you are. But my mom thought you should meet the people who would be working with her on this project—if you decide to go that route. They're from small businesses all over Williamtown."

Not the time to have things out, though, so all he could do was make the best of it.

"I'm officially impressed. Can you make introductions?"

"Sure."

Her voice was stilted and formal, and he let go of her, his fingers curling in an effort to remove the sensation. But it was still there, along with a pressure in the center of his chest. The last thing he needed to deal with was his unusual reaction to her.

With her hair pulled back and small diamonds in her earlobes, she looked cool and chic and not at all affected by his touch.

Sasha led him over to a woman he immediately recognized as her mother. Tall and slender, the similarities between them were uncanny. If he didn't know any better, he'd say this was Sasha's sister rather than her mom. It gave him a glimpse of what she would look like in the future.

Not that it was something he needed to know.

"Mom, this is Dr. Edwards. Dr. Edwards, this is Tessi James."

"Call me Nate, please. Sasha does. Normally, that is." He wondered if their kiss had somehow set them back a few steps. Or maybe because of how abrupt he'd been in his answer over Marie's doll. Whatever it was, he missed hearing his name on her lips.

"Okay, Nate. Everyone calls me Tessi, so you might as well too."

He forced his attention away from the woman's daughter. "Great. So who have you brought with you today, Tessi?"

As the woman introduced each member of her entourage, Nate found his attention kept returning to Sasha, who was fidgeting next to him. Okay, maybe she wasn't as unaffected as he'd thought. Or worse, maybe that kiss had made things unbearably awkward for her. He could talk to her after this, and see if he could fix things. Or maybe take her out to lunch, depending on how long the meeting took. He wasn't sure why he felt the need to make things right, but the thought of things staying like they were… Well, he didn't like it. And he had no idea why.

"Nice to meet all of you. Let's pull some chairs into a circle, and you can tell me what you have in mind for the fund-raiser."

There were two florists, ten people from various food industries in Williamtown, a couple of people from janitorial services and the rest were a jumble of party planners, organizers and a company that provided plating and cutlery.

He hadn't been lying when he'd said he was impressed. When Sasha had said her mom cooked and made wedding cakes and the like, he'd had his doubts over whether she could handle an event of this size…but with all of these people? He could see it unfolding before his eyes. And they would probably save quite a bit of money by having everything sourced locally.

Tessi and her group had pictures on their phones of what they envisioned doing with the event.

"Wow. You pulled all of this together in this short a period of time?"

Tessi nodded. "Between us, we have decades of experience to draw from."

"Can you send these to me?" He gave the group his cell phone number. "With your permission I'll print some of these off and present them at the meeting tonight. If you're sure you're all available. Tessi, if you could come and represent your group and answer any questions…?"

"Yes, of course." She gave him a grin. "We've also drawn up a budget of expenses for you to look over."

"Yes, I'll be happy to."

They talked a bit more about the particulars. An hour later, he was convinced. And satisfied. He sent Sasha a smile and mouthed, "Thank you."

She smiled back and nodded.

They stood and Sasha hugged her mom and thanked the rest of the crew, telling her mom that she wanted to stay behind and talk to Dr. Edwards for a few minutes but would see her at home later this evening. Then they were gone.

Nate turned to her. "So we're back to Dr. Edwards and Dr. James, are we?"

Her mouth quirked to the side. "No, I just don't want my mom to get any funny ideas."

"Does she get ideas about all the men you're on a first-name basis with?"

"No, of course not, but we're not simply on first name…"

Her voice trailed away, reminding him

that, like him, she probably didn't kiss every person she worked with. For some reason, that sent a burst of warmth through him. Although he remembered her talking to a male nurse at Saint Victoria Hospital, and at the time had wondered if there was something between the pair. But she wouldn't have kissed him the way she had, if that was the case. Right?

He decided maybe it was better if they didn't go back to his office after all. Especially after what had happened there. He could think of somewhere a whole lot safer.

Glancing down at her feet and seeing casual sandals that went with her long gauzy skirt, he asked. "Are your feet all recovered?"

She wiggled her toes. "Yep, as good as new."

"How do you feel about a walk on the beach then? We can talk as we go."

"Sure."

Was it his imagination, or did she seem relieved that he hadn't suggested his office?

Nate pushed through a nearby exit, guiding her over to the long boardwalk that led away from the hotel. Strolling along it, she glanced at him. "So did you really like what they had to say?"

"Are you kidding? It's fantastic, better than I'd even hoped."

She smiled. "There's even a DJ here in town who can probably do the music, if that's something you'd be interested in."

"Yes. I'd love to talk with him or her." He looked out over the sea. "Your mom has quite a bit of influence here."

"I don't know that it's influence as much as having grown up with most of those people. It's a little different here than in Boston or New York or any of the big cities in the States. There are fewer people moving in and out, so friends and neighbors spend a lifetime getting to know each other."

He liked the thought of knowing a group of people that well. At least the idea of it. How well could you really know anyone? He'd grown up with his parents, only to discover how little he understood them. And how little they understood him.

Shaking away that thought, he came to the end of the boardwalk and stepped out onto the sand.

"You're going to ruin your shoes," she murmured.

He glanced down at his shiny black dress shoes. "They've been out here more than once. As long as you don't throw me into the water, we should be good."

"Throw you into the water? Really?" A lightness came into her voice that made him relax. Maybe they'd get through that incident in his office unscathed after all. She was really the most surprising woman. Some of the women he'd been with had been quick to try to get a second date, but Sasha hadn't done anything to indicate she wanted anything from him. Not a kiss. Not anything else.

Their eyes met. Got hung up. And he wondered if he was somehow wrong.

Then she stepped onto the beach and moved away from him. He stopped to strip his shoes and socks off, carrying them in one hand.

"You come out here often," she said.

"Why do you say that?"

"Your feet are as tanned as the rest of you."

Her assessment was right on target as far as him liking to be out here.

"I do sit and watch the ocean sometimes, but not here."

"Where? Another beach?"

"No, I'll show you. It's about a fifteen-minute trek, though, do you have time?"

"I do, actually."

They walked until they arrived at a sheltered cove that none of the hospital staff knew about. As far as Nate knew, he was the only person who ever came out here. It was around a curve and well hidden from anyone walking along the beach. "This is the spot."

Sasha moved closer to the water. "It's beautiful. I can see why you like to come out here." Lowering herself onto the sand, she kicked off her sandals and stretched her legs out in front of her, tossing her skirt over them. She'd polished her toes this time and the bright fuchsia drew his eyes toward the high arch of her foot—the smooth, silky-looking legs below the white fabric. She was gorgeous. And he was beginning to think her beauty really was more than skin deep. Working with her on the accident victim had shown him that she was skilled and caring, jumping in to help even when she could have left to go home.

The discovery made him uneasy. Because it put that kiss in a completely different light. And Nate liked categorizing things so that they fit neatly into the box he'd made for himself. Of things he did and didn't allow himself to think or do.

He was glad he'd suggested coming here rather than inviting her out to lunch like he'd planned to. The sound of the water lapping at the beach was soothing. And he didn't really want anyone to hear what he had to say.

"I think I owe you an apology."

"You do? About what?" Her head turned toward him, face registering her surprise. "And please don't say it was about the kiss. It was a mistake. I think we both realize that."

He pulled up short. Okay, she'd beat him to it. He should be elated. But instead, something made him change tack and pretend the kiss wasn't even important enough to discuss. "No, not about that. I was kind of short with you that night."

"You were? I don't remember you being short."

Was it possible he was mistaken? Or was she just saying that? Well, either way, he'd started down this path and he was going to see it through to the bitter end. And he realized it was true. He did want to explain why he'd acted the way he did.

"You asked about that doll on my shelf, and I cut you off."

"Ah. That. You had every right to. I was prying, even though I didn't mean to." She blinked, then a frown puckered her brow. "Oh! Do you have a daughter?"

Her glance went to his hand. Damn. "No. I'm not married. I certainly wouldn't have kissed you if I was. And I don't have any children, here or in the States." Did she really think he was someone who would cheat on someone? That stung and he wasn't sure why.

"And… I'm prying again."

"No, you're not. Really." He just hadn't expected her to jump to that conclusion. "The doll belonged to a patient."

"And she gave it to you? How sweet. Those dolls are normally treasured possessions."

Yes. They were. This was going to be harder than he'd thought. "No. *She* didn't give it to me. Her parents did. Afterward."

She looked at him, head tilting. Then the softness of her face changed in an instant. "Oh, Nate, I'm so sorry. I had no idea."

"She was one of my patients when I was here with Medicine Around the World. It was after Hurricane Regan and was my first time on the island."

"That was a terrible time for Saint Victoria. So many businesses and lives wiped out. Parts of the island still haven't fully recovered. Was your patient injured in the hurricane?"

"No. At least that wasn't why her parents brought her to me. She had a persistent fever, was jaundiced and was very ill. Saint Victoria Hospital was in shambles at the time, and we only had rudimentary medical supplies with us. I treated her for hepatitis, but she just got worse. And the blood work I sent off didn't get back before she..."

Sasha's hand reached over and gripped his. "How awful. Did you find out what it was?"

"Yes. And that was the kicker. She had schistosomiasis."

She blinked, and there was a long pause while she stared at him. "God, Nate. That was *you*."

Confusion ran through him before a sense of horror kicked him in the gut. Were people talking about the foreign doctor who let a young child die?

Her hand squeezed his. "Not long after the hurricane, there was a campaign to test the water and try to find out where there were concentrations of the parasite. And doctors looked carefully at any case of swimmers' rash or symptoms of hepatitis or unexplained infections. They actually found a couple of children in a family with the chronic gastrointestinal form of schistosomiasis and were able to treat them with praziquantel. Both children lived. It's not as common in Saint Victoria as it is in some of the other tropical climates, but obviously it can kill. Even here." She leaned closer, and bumped his shoulder with hers. "You may not know it, but you're probably the reason those two kids are still alive."

Nate had actually sent his own money to the island anonymously asking it to be earmarked for the prevention and treatment of schistosomiasis.

"It was my first time out of the country as a doctor, and I'd never seen a case before. I always felt if I'd identified it earlier..."

"You couldn't have known and it would have been too late by then, anyway. Our island was struggling on a lot of different fronts at that time." Her fingers twined with his. "Believe me—her parents would not have given you that doll if they weren't extremely grateful to you. If they felt you hadn't done everything possible to save their child."

"I would have done almost anything to save her."

"I think you did everything you could have." She studied him. "What was her name?"

"Marie." A hard twinge went through his jaw, and he forced his teeth to unclench. He didn't often say her name out loud.

There was silence for a few seconds, then Sasha said, "I'm glad you kept her doll."

"It's a reminder. She's why I came back to Saint Victoria."

"I'm glad for that too." Her voice lowered. "Even if it was for those reasons."

Was she really? He'd gotten the idea she wasn't thrilled about him being there. Actually, she'd pretty much admitted it to him. And although he should have been able to let it roll off his back, her prickliness when they'd first met had bothered him. And he wasn't sure why.

Was she changing her mind about him? Maybe. They were back on a first-name basis again. And he felt better after confiding in her.

Just then a sound hit his ears and a rogue wave rushed toward them before he could warn her, sloshing over their legs and knocking Sasha flat on her back. She sputtered, and he went to yank her upright before realizing she wasn't struggling, she was laughing.

"*Bondye mwen*, what just happened?"

He leaned over her, chuckling at the look on her face. "*Bondye mwen*, indeed."

"Sorry, the language just slips out sometimes. You know what it means?"

"After three years, I should. Besides, *my God* kind of comes through in any language.

And I like those little slipups." Maybe because he'd pretty much had that same thought. Only it hadn't been about the wave. It was about how she looked right now, with her hair plastered to her head and her skirt… Hell, the thing was almost transparent.

Her eyes widened and she sat up in a rush. "Oh, no. Your shoes."

"What about them?"

She waved her hand. "Well, one is here and one is…down there."

"Ah, hell." He leaped up, hearing her laughter as he jogged down to the low point of the water where his errant shoe was tumbling in the surf. He snatched it up, just as another wave crashed over his knees almost knocking him down. He looked up at where she was sitting and saw she'd made no move to stand up. She was holding her stomach as laughter poured out of her.

Suddenly, he felt carefree, loved that she could just get flattened by a wave and laugh about it rather than getting angry at her clothes being soaked. He tried to picture his mom in this kind of situation.

She definitely wouldn't have been doubled over in mirth.

Reaching her side, he grabbed his other shoe and then her sandals and threw them out of the sea's reach. Then he dropped back by her side. "So you find that funny, do you?"

"Yes. Very." The laughter came again. "If you could have seen yourself running toward the water, your pant legs dragging around your ankles. What kind of chief of staff are you, anyway?"

"A very wet one. I could ask the same of you." He leaned closer, murmuring, "What kind of doctor are you?"

The question hung in the air for a few seconds, before she said, "The kind who can laugh at herself."

"Really? It seems you were laughing more at me, than at yourself."

Her brows went up. "And you have a problem with that?"

"No. No problem at all." In fact, he liked it. Very, very much.

This time the kiss wasn't impulsive. Wasn't a spur-of-the-moment thing. He'd thought about it. Thought about all the reasons why it was a bad idea. And then Nate Edwards leaned over and did it anyway.

It was even better this time. The kiss. The setting.

The laughter.

She hadn't laughed that hard with a man in…well, forever.

It made having his mouth on hers that much sweeter.

He laid her back in the sand and followed her down, and right now she didn't care if the water rushed up and covered her head. If that happened, she would keep on kissing him for as long as she could hold her breath.

The heat of his body penetrated her wet clothes, her skin, reaching the innermost part of her. Sasha did not kiss men she barely knew. But here she was, rushing into uncharted territory, just like that wave that had crashed into them.

Only this was more powerful than that wave. And unlike Nate's shoe, it was unlikely she was going to catch herself before she tumbled into something even more dangerous. Something that wouldn't be as easy to pull free from.

But right now, she just didn't care.

Wrapping her arms around his neck, she pulled him closer, her tongue touching his, tasting coffee and mint and… Nate.

One of his legs slid between hers as he closed the gap between them, and something nudged against the outside of her thigh. Her insides melted.

She wanted him. Here in the sand, under the sky.

"Sasha…"

The sound of her name made her open her eyes. His were deep and dark and full of all of the things she was feeling. Another wave went over her, sliding between their bodies, the juxtaposition of the cool water and the heat of his skin making her nipples pucker.

He kissed her again as the water receded. It was long and drawn out, making her breathless for more. Then he pulled away slightly. "You're going to drown if we stay here."

"Mmm, I can hold my breath for a very long time. So I don't think I care."

"But I do."

He stood, and she was just about to protest, when he reached down and swung her up in his arms. "Oh!"

"Yes, oh." He chuckled before walking with purpose down toward the water, moving sideways in a way that avoided them taking the brunt of the waves.

A heady sense of need went through her. He wasn't stopping. He was doing the opposite: making it possible for them to do more. Feel more. Explore more. He carried her farther out in this private slice of paradise, until the water covered her bottom and sent delicious sensations through her. Then he set her down on her feet.

He kissed her. Recklessly. With a passion and fervor that rivaled anything she'd ever felt before. Then he slowly turned her away from him, facing the shore as his fingers edged under her light top, under her bra, palms sliding over her breasts in a way that drove the air from her lungs. She pushed into his touch, with a soft cry, glad it was muted by the sounds of the sea. It didn't matter. No one would see them here. Her hands rounded his strong thighs and closed over his butt, dragging him closer, until he was nestled tight against her.

Nate leaned down and nipped at her ear. "You're driving me crazy, Sash."

No crazier than he was driving her. She hoped he had a condom somewhere on him, although she felt like she would die if she didn't have him however she could get him.

One of his arms dipped beneath the water, coming up under her skirt and bunching it around her legs. His fingers found her lacy undergarment and he slid against her, making her instinctively move toward the hard heat she felt behind her. He pushed against her, groaning as his fingers found her, brushing over that sensitive part of her and cupping her.

"Do you want this, sweetheart? If you don't, please tell me now."

"Yes. I want it." The words came out with a need that almost made her cringe. Until he growled against her ear, pushing her panties down her legs.

She stepped out of them not caring if they were lost forever to the sea. It seemed kind of fitting since she was finding herself lost to it too. Then his fingers were on her flesh, teasing, squeezing, trailing across her folds and blotting out every other thought but what was happening to her. He dipped inside her with a suddenness that made her clench around his finger.

Yes. She wanted it. Way too much.

"Hell. You're going to have to help me."

He withdrew and somehow, from his wallet or his pocket or some secret place pulled a packet above the water and handed it to her. She pivoted toward him as she ripped the packet open and handed him the wrapper. He shoved it in his pocket just as her hands slid beneath the surface of the water. When she found him, he'd already released himself. All she had to do was. Slide. It. Slowly. On.

It was heavenly. Warm and heavy and, oh, so hard. She could explore him forever.

But as soon as she'd sheathed him, his hands scooped beneath her thighs, lifted her onto his hips. She twined her ankles beneath his butt.

With one palm pressed against the small of her back, he used his other hand to find her, entering her with one swift deep thrust.

"Ahh…" She pressed her face against his neck, panting against his skin as she absorbed the sensation of being stretched. So very full.

"Okay?"

"Yes. Oh, yes."

Supporting her butt, he began to move, thrusting slowly, the water providing the perfect medium for them. The push and pull of the waves echoed what was happening inside her. She licked salt from his neck, murmured in her own tongue against his lips, before allowing herself to slide back into the water, her body buoyed by the salt and sea currents.

She could see him above her moving, eyes on hers. The sight was hypnotic. She couldn't see where they were joined but could see the muscles under his shirt contract with each forward movement, could feel the result inside her.

"Sasha, I need...to...touch you." Each word was punctuated with a short thrust that made her push against him.

A luscious pressure was building inside her. "You are, Nate." She took a breath. "Just keep doing what you're doing."

His hands squeezed her ass as he pulled her harder against him with each stroke. Her legs tightened around him, adding her own rhythm in an effort to keep up with the demands of her flesh.

Suddenly one of his arms slid under her back, and he supported her, leaning forward and taking her nipple into his mouth, then sucking hard. She held on to his shoulders to keep herself from going under as she watched his mouth work its magic on her, his hair wet and dark and wild.

As wild as she felt inside.

She moved against him, the friction against sensitive areas of her body making any hope of drawing this out impossible.

Using her legs, she pumped herself on him, going faster and faster, watching as his head came up, eyes glazing.

And then she was there, her body tumbling and crashing and exploding, as a keening cry erupted from her throat.

Nate's own cry joined hers a few seconds

later as a frenzy of thrusts drove her even higher.

And then it was over. She lay on top of the water for a few seconds, her breath heaving, trying to push through the thick layer of sludge that seemed to have taken over her brain.

With one hand still behind her waist, he used his other hand to pull her upright until she was resting against him.

Neither one of them said anything for a few minutes. Then Nate eased free, and she closed her eyes in an attempt to blot out the truth: it was over. And she had no idea what to say.

He saved her from having to come up with something. "Are you okay?"

"Yes." She moistened her lips, almost dreading to hear his response. "You?"

"I think I just destroyed something."

She blinked at him in shock before realizing he was smiling. She smiled back at him, having no idea what he was talking about. "You did? What?"

"You were worried about my shoes. But neither one of us thought about this. Well I did. But I didn't care at the time."

He reached behind him and up out of the

sea came his wallet. And it was streaming with water.

And suddenly she was laughing just like she'd been on the beach. This could have been the most awkward moment ever. And all Sasha felt was gratitude that he'd come up with the perfect icebreaker, even if his wallet had paid the price. She leaned forward and hugged him, putting every ounce of feeling she had into it as she thanked him in the only way she knew how.

And then she set her feet on the ground, and turned and trudged slowly toward shore.

CHAPTER SIX

SASHA DIDN'T MAKE the next gala meeting that
night, even though her mom did, bringing
with her an impressive presentation that Nate
added to what they'd already sent him. And
as it had been at the last meeting, the vote
was unanimous that they let Tessi James's
team head up the food and decorations. All
they had to provide were the venue and the
speakers. And that was the easy part.

And although he was glad things had gone
in Tessi's favor, his mind was on the woman's
daughter during most of the meeting.

She'd seemed to be okay after their...
don't say it... But the words *sex on the beach*
surged through his mind anyway. He barely
refrained from rolling his eyes in front of
everyone.

Maybe she wasn't okay though. And he
had something in his office that belonged
to her. He just wasn't quite sure how to get

them back to her. He could mail them. But that seemed worse than handing them to her in person, somehow.

Except how? And where? Was there even a comfortable way for that exchange to take place?

He could just throw them away, but then she might wonder what had happened to them or worry that they might wash up on the shore somewhere.

He adjourned the meeting, and as far as he knew everything was set in place for the gala.

Tessi came up to him afterward, and he tensed, wondering if Sasha had talked to her about what happened. He forced a smile.

"I just wanted to say thank you for letting us do the food and service for the fundraiser."

"I should be thanking you. And Sasha, of course. She's the one who ultimately thought of it."

The woman nodded as if her thoughts were elsewhere. "She hasn't had it easy. First her dad and then that fiasco with Austin."

"Austin?" Nate knew about her dad and his death, but the other name wasn't familiar.

The woman frowned. "A man she dated at Harvard. He was rich and pretended to like her. But as soon as he got what he wanted—a job at a prestigious hospital—he dumped her. After five years of dating."

Shock rolled through him. She'd never mentioned having a relationship with anyone while in medical school. And somehow it seemed inappropriate to be talking about this with her mother. Especially since a wave of guilt had just knocked him for a loop.

Did she equate him with this Austin person?

No. They'd never talked about dating. And she'd acted like what had happened was all in good fun. But maybe it wasn't. Maybe on some level she expected him to...

To what?

Start a relationship with her? He hadn't dated seriously since Tara. And he'd had no desire to do so.

No. He thought over what had happened, and there'd been no hint that Sasha felt anything more for him than physical attraction. Which was good. Because that's all he felt for her too.

Right?

Of course. They barely knew each other.

And yet he'd told her about Marie. He told other people about the doll, but he rarely discussed it in the kind of detail he'd shared with her. And he'd never told Tara about it at all.

And Sasha had never once mentioned Austin.

"I'm sorry. I had no idea that had happened."

"She doesn't talk about it." Tessi's eyes closed. "And she would be very angry if she knew I'd shared it with you. I'm sorry. Would you mind…?"

"I won't say a word."

"Thank you so much. I don't even know why I said anything." Even as she said the words, worry lined the woman's face.

He tried to erase the concern. "You have a very special daughter."

"I know. I only wish she knew how much people think of her."

Nate thought of her entirely too much. But he needed to make sure that stopped here and now. She'd already been hurt by one man, who according to Tessi had toyed with her emotions and then cut her off without a word. Kind of like his parents had done with him?

Well, he had no intention of adding his name to a list of people who had hurt her.

So what was he going to do about it?

Maybe talk to her. Go have that lunch

they'd never had. And do what? Lay her undergarment on her salad plate?

Hell, he shouldn't even be thinking about that with her mom standing right in front of him.

So he just added his own thought to hers. "I wish she did too. But people like Sasha aren't normally aware of just how important they are."

"That's the truth." Tessi smiled and reached up to pat his face. "But I have an idea that you do."

Then she turned and walked away, leaving Nate standing there in shock. Had Sasha said something to her after all? Or was her mom simply reading signs that weren't there.

He was going to go with the latter. And if he was the one giving off some kind of vibe he was going to have to cut it off at the knees. And if it was Sasha?

Well, he was going to have to make sure she understood exactly where they stood. And that was nowhere.

One of the nurses came in and interrupted his thoughts. "Mr. Blankenship would like to meet with you and talk about his wife's skin cancer surgery."

"Of course. I'll be right there."

Merriam Blankenship was an award-winning actress who'd starred in countless movies. She was at the height of her career, only to have it almost sidelined by a melanoma diagnosis on her left cheek. With what could be a disfiguring surgery looming on the horizon, she'd chosen to come to The Island Clinic to have the removal and reconstruction done. Nate and the plastic surgeon who worked out of the clinic had warned them it could take up to a year. Tendrils of the cancer had infiltrated the bone below it and it was going to be tricky to get clean margins, much less leave a smooth symmetrical result. There would be bone and skin grafts, and there was always the risk of nerve damage.

But this was what he was here for. Their plastic surgeon was one of the best in the world. And the Blankenships had already poured a huge sum into the Saint Victoria Foundation. The cost of privacy, they'd said. Nate had laid the base for that private foundation, using his own trust fund. The least he could do was guarantee the Blankenships got what they wanted.

His parents were top in the plastic-surgery field, and maybe he should have consulted with them on this case, but he couldn't bring himself to make that call.

There were only a few doctors at The Island Clinic who actually knew that Jackson and Sheryl Edwards were his parents. They'd worked on many A-list clients just like Merriam Blankenship. But Merriam didn't want to do this under the spotlight of Los Angeles, and he couldn't blame her.

So putting Sasha firmly out of his mind, he headed to the elevator and the second floor, where The Island Clinic's newest high-profile patient was waiting.

Sasha was taking a break in the staff lounge, eating a forbidden Danish when Nate walked in. She tried to banish the look of guilt that she knew was splashed across her face.

"Hey, can I have a word?"

She still had a big bite of the pastry in her mouth, so forced herself to chew. And chew and chew before finally swallowing. If this had to do with what had happened in the sea yesterday, she was going to wish she'd choked on that Danish.

"Um sure." She glanced at the chair next to her.

But Nate didn't sit down. He just stood there for a minute. The sugar in the pastry she'd just eaten soured in her stomach.

Another doctor came into the room and

took one look at them and quickly grabbed a water and excused himself.

Great. Just what she wanted. To look like she was having some cozy interlude with the chief of staff from The Island Clinic.

A place she'd scoffed about to Patty.

But hadn't she had that cozy interlude? Down by the beach?

Yes. But she didn't want anyone else to know about it. Not even Patty. Surely he hadn't...

"Er...no one knows about..."

"I was just going to ask you the same thing." His face held a seriousness she hadn't seen since they'd operated on that accident victim at The Island Clinic.

He thought she'd told someone? "No, I haven't said anything. To anyone."

"You didn't come to the meeting last night, and your mom said something odd to me."

"She did?"

"I just wanted to make sure it didn't have anything to do with what happened."

What had her mother said now? "I didn't say anything to her. At all. And I won't."

"Okay, thanks." A beat went by. "Do you think we could have lunch? Where no one from the hospital has a chance to overhear?"

Great. He was going to make sure she knew that the sea sex meant nothing.

Sea sex. That sounded like something out of an old tongue twister. *Susie sells sea sex by the seashore.*

Sasha laughed, but it came out half-choked. That damned Danish! That's what she got for sneaking stuff she wasn't supposed to have.

Like Nate?

Her laughter dried up in a hurry. "Sorry. I just always seem to get caught doing something I shouldn't."

"We…didn't get caught."

"Not that. This." She pushed the plate forward. "I swore off sugar."

"Ah." He actually smiled. "So if I offered to buy you a sugarless lunch, would you accept?"

"Why?"

"I just wanted to make sure we're on the same page about things."

She stiffened her back. "I'm pretty sure we are." Was he expecting her to cry and beg him not to throw her away?

Too late. She'd already done that with Austin. Without the begging part. She was not anxious to repeat that mistake. Which was why she *should* go to lunch with him. If only to assure him that she had no designs on his person or anything else.

Liar. She did have designs on his person. But only in the physical sense. As for the emotional sense she was free and clear. At least she hoped she was. If not, she was going to make sure she reached that point. So maybe she should hear him out. It would drive home the fact that he was not interested in her.

"Maybe. But I still would like to go somewhere where we can have a little privacy. I have something for you."

He did? Her heart leaped in her chest. *Stop it, Sasha! He doesn't mean it that way.*

"This was actually supposed to be my lunch break. So maybe somewhere 'sugarless' would be better."

"Okay, I know a place down the street that pretty much fits that bill."

A few minutes later they were seated in a place that was known for its conch soup and fried seafood. She wasn't sure it qualified as being healthier than her Danish, but it was delicious. And she'd eaten here more than once. She was actually surprised that Nate hadn't taken her somewhere fancier. Someplace that fit in with his fancy clinic.

She frowned at the thought, pushing it from her head.

Studying the menu for a minute, she chose a bowl of the soup and half a sandwich, while Nate ordered the soup plus a plate of fried clam strips and chips, with a side of cocktail sauce.

When their food arrived, Nate pulled a small paper bag out of his pocket and handed it to her under the table. "I needed to return this, but didn't want to do it at either of our hospitals."

"Return…" She placed the bag next to her plate and started to open it, when he placed his hand over hers. "I don't think you're going to want to do that in here."

Suddenly she knew what it was and her face blazed with heat. She'd totally forgotten about them, had assumed they'd been swept away with the tide. Evidently, he'd retrieved them, somehow. Or had they appeared on the beach near the clinic later? The heat in her face turned into an inferno. "Um…thanks. I'm glad I didn't litter. You could have just tossed them though." She shoved the bag in the deepest darkest recesses of her purse. Had he washed them? The thought of him pulling them out of the washing machine was even worse. Or of them being plastered against his own laundry and him having to slowly peel them apart. More heat drummed at her temples. A very different kind of heat.

"I thought about it, but then wondered if you'd worry about what happened to them. Or the thought that you'd 'littered'..." he smiled as he reused her term "...or that they'd reappear somewhere more public. And you walked back to the clinic so fast afterward that there was no time to hand them to you."

He was right. She had made a beeline all the way back to the boardwalk and beyond. Once her senses returned, she hadn't wanted to dissect what had happened, just figured if they didn't talk about it, they were both free to let it drop.

Like she'd done with her underwear.

Sayè!

"Okay, well, thanks." Her appetite had suddenly deserted her. "Is this why you wanted to bring me here?"

"Partly. But I also wanted to apologize."

"Oh, please. Don't." He'd already apologized for the other stuff. She couldn't bear it if he went into some huge monologue about how badly he felt about them tumbling around in the waves too. "I don't regret what happened. Any of it."

Really? *Really?*

Hadn't she regretted it so much that she hadn't been able to show her face at the meeting last night, afraid she'd be undressing him with her eyes the whole time? She hadn't actually gotten to see much of him in the water. But the parts that she'd felt…

"I don't regret it either. But I also don't want it to affect our working relationship. And I certainly don't want to be the reason why you…"

He seemed to be struggling to say something. But he needn't bother. "Listen. I went into that water knowing exactly where things stood, if that's what you're trying to get at. I don't expect anything of you, and I don't think you expect anything of me. I haven't been with anyone in a long time, and things just got…carried away. But it was nice and I…enjoyed it."

The words were ludicrous. She made it sound like she'd read a pleasant book.

His lips twitched. "Good to know it was *nice*. But I also wanted you to know that I don't make a habit of sleeping with colleagues. I know how messy that can get. How much it can hurt when things don't turn out the way you expect them to."

Something in his face. The way he was avoiding her eyes right now. Was that…pity?

Oh, hell, no. "Exactly what did my mother say to you?"

"Say?"

"Don't even act like you don't know what I'm talking about."

His smile was crooked. And worried. "You two are far too much alike, did you know that? She made me promise to keep it to myself."

This took the cake. Actually she should have finished that Danish. She could use a shot of sugar right now. "Did she guess about...you know? Is that why she said something?"

"I don't think so. I thought at first maybe you'd told her and that's why she brought up Austin."

At the sound of that name, her soup curdled in her stomach. "I'm pretty sure she would have confronted me, if she'd guessed."

"Well, I came to the same conclusion, that it was a genuine slip of the tongue. It came out after she mentioned your dad and how hard his loss was."

Sasha took a deep breath, her anger dissipating immediately. "Yes, I can see her linking the two. I'm just embarrassed that she brought him up. I was stupid and naive, back then, and had never been around men with money before."

"Whether he had money or not shouldn't have made any difference. What the man did was wrong. And I wanted to make sure I hadn't inadvertently hurt you, as well."

It *had* been pity. But hadn't she felt a trace of that when he'd told her about Marie? About how broken he'd been by her death?

Maybe it wasn't pity. Maybe it was just... compassion. Understanding.

"You didn't hurt me. I knew what was what when we went into that water. Now, if you had professed your undying love for me only to retract it a few days later, I might have cut you up and fed you to the fish. But you didn't. And I didn't. So it's all good."

Even if he *had* said he loved her, she wouldn't have believed him. She was far too wise to be taken in by pretty words nowadays. Fortunately he'd not tossed any her way.

That made her smile. "Did your wallet end up being ruined?"

"More or less. It was fun explaining to my bank and creditors how my credit cards got lost in the sea."

"Will they reissue everything?"

"Yep. I should have them in a few days."

"I'm glad. And your shoes?"

"They dried out. A little buffing, and they should be passable again."

Her smile widened. She felt kind of like his shoes. A little buffing here and there and she should be passable again too. Right now, though, she still felt just a little vulnerable and quick to jump to conclusions whenever he said something. "I'm glad. And I'm very glad that part of the beach is so private."

Which made her wonder if he'd towed some other woman over to his "secret spot" and done the same thing. Except his earlier words made her think that he hadn't. At least not one of his colleagues. For that she was glad.

And if that first wave hadn't hit, they probably wouldn't have wound up in the predicament they had. At least they had an excuse for both of them returning soaked. She was pretty sure they weren't the first people who had been surprised by one of those crazy waves.

Luckily, once Nate had caught up with her, he'd sneaked her into one of the hotel rooms and let her dry her clothes and hair with one of the handheld hair dryers. She assumed he'd done the same in another room. Of course they did have an apartment block for the staff, from what she'd heard, so maybe he lived in one of them. Although he'd been wearing the same clothes when he came back to check on her. She'd driven her car over, so she'd hurried away before he had a chance to say much.

"I am, as well. And that we opted not to put cameras on any of the beaches out of respect for some of our more sensitive patients."

Yikes, she hadn't even thought about cameras. Surely he wouldn't have carried her into the water if there had been any. Of course it would have saved her from the embarrassing moment of having her underwear passed to her under the table.

But she'd told him the truth. She didn't regret going into that water. The experience had been exhilarating—freeing in a way she couldn't describe—and she'd probably never do anything like it again. Someday when she was a granny she'd probably think about that day with pride.

Unless she was never a grandmother.

Okay, Sasha. Not something you need to think about right now.

She spooned the last bit of conch soup into her mouth. Funny how what had tasted like cardboard a few moments earlier now tasted pretty darned good.

"How was your conch?"

"It's never failed to please."

The words *And how was I?* sang through her head. But of course she was never ever going to ask him that question.

"My mom actually gave them the recipe for the soup."

His brows went up in a way she was beginning to recognize. "You're kidding."

"I'm not. I hear she's planning on making it for the gala. It was my grandmother's recipe, originally."

He leaned forward. "Listen. I really need to thank you for suggesting we hire out to local companies. I think this year's fundraiser is going to be a big hit with the folks who attend."

"I hope so. I wondered after I suggested it. I hope they don't hate it all. You're taking a risk by agreeing."

"I think I can safely say the people who come are going to love everything about it. Some of them might never want to leave Saint Victoria."

"Like you?"

He smiled. "Yes. Like me."

And just like that, they were on ground

that felt more stable and less like quicksand. Somehow knowing that he never wanted to leave made her heart feel lighter than it had in the last couple of days. There'd been a tiny part of her that wondered what his plans for the future were. Well, it sounded like he had every intention of staying for the foreseeable future. "You know, I hear they have a great crème brûlée here."

"I thought you were swearing off sugar."

"I am. But since I already ruined my resolution with the Danish back at the staff lounge, I might as well hold off on renewing that vow until tomorrow."

He raised his hand to signal their waiter. "And that sounds like the best plan I've heard all day."

CHAPTER SEVEN

Was that lacy underwear still in her purse?

Nate spied Sasha just as he was wheeling Bill Waddel, their heart attack patient, through the double doors of the ER.

"They said you were coming through here. I'm so glad to see you."

The low, husky words should have made his chest tighten, except Sasha's eyes weren't on him, they were on Bill.

"I'm feeling much better. I wanted to thank you and Dr. Edwards for everything you did."

She smiled. "I think the cardiologist over at The Island Clinic is the one you should thank. We were short-staffed when you arrived and our cardiologist was stuck in surgery. It looks like they got you all patched up though."

"Two stents later, yes. I still have to go through cardiac rehab. I'm sure losing weight and eating better will be on the menu, but I'm willing to do anything to make sure I live to see my first grandchild who's due next month."

Only then did she glance up at Nate. The smile was still on her face, but she seemed a little more stiff than she had at the restaurant. It had been a couple of days since he'd seen her, though; he'd been busy trying to get things for the gala nailed down. And he'd heard that Marcus Warren, the doctor from Saint Victoria Hospital who'd been taking care of an ill relative, was back at work as of yesterday, so they hadn't needed him as much.

"Don't let me forget. I have something for you," she said.

She did? Those were almost the exact same words he'd used when he'd talked to her a couple of days ago. He hadn't left a piece of clothing in the sea, though.

Just the thought sent memories sliding through the deepest recesses of his brain. With it, came a question. Had the condom done its job even with everything so…wet? As in the sea water?

It had still been in place afterward, so everything pointed to it having effectively done its job, but it was new territory for him. He'd never dragged anyone into the ocean before. Not even Tara.

"Okay. I was just taking Bill to meet his therapy team here at Saint Victoria Hospital, since it's closer to where he lives."

"That makes sense. Our cardiac team is really good at what they do, including rehab."

Was there a note of defensiveness in her voice? She'd seemed wary that first day he'd come in to help, but he'd thought they'd made it past all of that stuff. There had been that kiss. And the sea.

So why was he feeling like they'd taken several steps backward? The hospitals weren't in competition with each other. He wanted The Island Clinic to be an enhancement of what Saint Victoria Hospital was doing. An addition. Not take the place of it. Maybe that was something he needed to work on.

"Good to know," Bill said.

His voice was still a touch weak, but after what he'd been through it was to be expected.

Nate glanced at her. "Do you have time to walk with us?"

"I do. Let's go. Cardiac Rehab is on this floor actually, so you won't have to worry with elevators or anything. And there's a separate entrance, so you'll be able to park near it and walk in. I'll show you where."

Nate had forgotten that the unit had its own entrance. Since it was at the back of the hospital, it made sense that they wouldn't want patients with more vulnerable health issues having to walk long distances.

They headed down the long corridor, making two turns before reaching glass doors with a sign reading, "Welcome to Saint Victoria Hospital Rehab. We'll kick your behinds…in the best possible way." It was punctuated with a smiley face sitting at some kind of weight machine.

Bill laughed. "I'm not sure how much kicking I can take. But I'll give it a shot."

While Sasha opened the door, Nate wheeled Bill in, heading for the reception desk. They got checked in, and he made sure Bill had someone picking him up. Sasha leaned down and gave their patient a hug. "Don't be a stranger. Let me know when you're here, and if I'm free I'll drop in to see you."

"I will. Thanks again for everything. Both of you."

Nate waited until Sasha caught up with him. "So you said you had something for me?"

"My mom sent over some conch soup. It's

in the refrigerator of the staff lounge. So it'll need to be heated up, obviously. She wanted you to taste it to make sure it's suitable."

"I already had some the day we went out to lunch. She doesn't have to send over a sample of everything. But I'll enjoy the soup. Tell her thank you."

"I will."

"So, I wasn't sure if you were worried about the aftermath of what happened. But I wanted to let you know that everything was still in place afterward."

"Still in place?"

"The protection." He lowered his voice.

"Oh." Her eyes widened. "Ooh. I didn't even think about it. But thanks for letting me know. I probably should be on the Pill, but I don't…well, there's not really a need as I…"

"I get it. It's okay. I just didn't want you panicking. But if for some reason, you are… late…"

She nodded. "I'll let you know. But like you said, as long as everything was still there it should be fine. There were no oils or sunscreens involved."

"Right."

He decided to change the subject. "You know you don't have to defend Saint Victoria Hospital every time I'm around."

"Defend it, what do you mean?"

"Just that when you were talking about the cardiac rehab center, it sounded like you wanted to make sure I knew that it was up to snuff."

Her eyes squinched just a bit. "It came through, did it? Sorry. It's just a habit. Sometimes I wonder if people see us as second best."

"I've never heard anything but good things about the hospital, or I wouldn't have invested so much in it."

She gave a half shrug. "I think I know that up here," she pointed at her head, "but in here, I'm not always so sure." With that, she pressed her hand to her chest.

He found the gesture touching somehow. And it had probably been hard for her to admit that. And he really did know what she meant. Firsthand, actually. "I get it. Sometimes you can feel that way regardless."

"What do you mean?"

Hell. He wasn't sure why he'd said that, except at her words, the image of his parents presenting that plaque came to mind. And their expressions when he'd been forced to tell them that he wasn't ever going to join their practice because he wasn't going to specialize in plastic surgery. They'd had this look on their faces. Like they suddenly weren't even sure he was their child.

"Nothing, really. I'm sure we've just all felt that way at some time or other. Not good enough, I mean."

"Yes, I'm sure we all have."

She drew the words out on a little sigh. Was she thinking of the man she'd dated at Harvard? What was his name? Austin, right? In trying to take the spotlight off himself, he may have just reminded Sasha of a painful time in her life.

Before he could try to think of a way to pull the words in a different direction, she spoke up.

"I actually have the next week off. I was wondering..." She shook her head. "Never mind."

"No. What?"

She stopped and looked up at him. "Well, you mentioned me sounding defensive about Saint Victoria Hospital. Maybe it's not so much defensive as it is protective. So... maybe I could spend a few days at The Island Clinic and see how things work over there. Like you did over here. Well...you didn't do it for that reason, but if there's something I could help with, maybe it would—"

"Help you see us with different eyes."

"Exactly."

He liked the idea. Not because it would give him more time to spend with her. Not at all. But they'd often had doctors from the hospital come over and work with them. He had a feeling that Sasha could be a powerful voice in their favor if he could win her over.

"I think that's a great idea. Let me know when you want to start and how many hours you want to put in each day, and we can put you somewhere…trauma, maybe?"

"How about Monday. I can float around. Maybe see a couple of surgeries done."

He was pretty sure one of Merriam Blankenship's reconstruction surgeries was coming up next week. It might be a good one for her to see. "We have a couple of nice observation areas. And I think I know a good one for you to watch. A melanoma that infiltrated a woman's cheekbone. She'll need pretty extensive repair work."

He'd have to get Merriam's permission for her to watch but as long as he assured her that it was educational and had nothing to do with her fame, she would probably be okay with it. Not even his parents' practice could afford patients the amount of privacy that The Island Clinic did. There were no cell phones allowed in certain areas of the clinic, even by staff members. And there were rigorous background checks and waivers that everyone signed. There was also a one-strike-you're-out policy. Nate would not hesitate to prosecute anyone who violated patient confidentiality.

The Island Clinic's very existence depended on its ability to keep its promise to its patients.

"That sounds interesting. I would love to watch."

"I'll join you. Let me find out exactly when it is, and I'll get back to you. In the meantime, if you want to come in on Monday, I can take you on rounds."

"Perfect. What time are rounds?"

"Eight. Do you want me to send the shuttle?"

"It's okay. I'll drive over. It'll make it easier on everyone."

They stopped at the staff lounge. "Let me get that container of soup for you."

"Thanks. Much appreciated." As he watched her duck into the room, he was buoyed by the thought of her seeing the clinic. It would be the perfect opportunity to see all that was right about his medical facility. And to change her mind about it, once and for all.

* * *

On Monday morning, Sasha went through the front doors of The Island Clinic and was met by the sound of screaming and people running in all directions. What the...?

Out of habit she started to race toward the sound, only to be stopped by someone at the reception desk. "I'm sorry. Can I help you?"

Of course she couldn't just jump in. No one knew who she was. "I'm Dr. James from Saint Victoria Hospital. I'm supposed to go on rounds with Dr. Edwards this morning."

"Oh, of course, he told me you were coming. Let me see if I can page him." The young woman was calm and serene, acting like there wasn't something terrible going on less than a hundred feet from her station.

"Can I help with something?"

This time the woman bit her lip. "I'm not sure... Let me see if I can find out." She put her ear to the phone and spoke in low tones to whoever was on the other end. Then she hung up.

"Dr. Edwards is on his way."

Still no reply to her original question. But the sounds were also dying down. She had to remember, this wasn't Saint Victoria Hospital. She couldn't just walk in and take charge like she was used to in her ER. But it was hard to shut off the part of her mind that said *run*! when she heard sounds of distress.

Nate came down the hallway, motioning her forward. He nodded at the receptionist. "Thanks, Jen."

Impressive. He knew her name. Although Saint Victoria Hospital's administrator probably knew most of the names at their hospital, as well. She just always expected to be met with snootiness here at The Island Clinic. So far she'd been proven wrong at every turn.

"What's happening?"

The screams had reduced to muffled crying.

"They're doing bandage changes on the melanoma patient that I told you about." He paused. "For someone who makes a living off her appearance… Well, it would be a shock to anyone."

"I can imagine." So it had to be someone famous. Patty had mentioned that a lot of well-known and well-heeled people came through The Island Clinic's doors. "Does that happen often?"

"Surgery?"

"No…screaming. Your receptionist was as cool as could be about it."

"No. It doesn't happen often. No more than any other hospital."

Touché. Saint Victoria Hospital had had its share of patients and families whose emotions got the better of them. And some for good reason. The hospital was not the happiest of places most of the time. Except for maybe in the obstetrics wing.

Which made her wonder. "Do you have obstetrics here?"

His eyes narrowed. "We do. Why?"

Too late, she realized he was probably remembering their earlier conversation about condoms. "I just wondered."

"Does this have anything to do with what we talked about?"

"Not at all." She decided to explain. "I was just thinking about how hospitals aren't necessarily a place of laughter. Except the maternity ward."

"That makes sense." His shoulders sank in what looked like relief. Well, why wouldn't he be relieved? He probably wouldn't be thrilled if someone he'd had a brief encounter with got pregnant. Visions of Austin came to mind. Would he have stayed with her, if she'd been expecting his child?

She couldn't think of a worse reason to be with someone you didn't love. And he hadn't loved her. That much was obvious. And looking back, it was probably for the best, although at the time she had felt used and humiliated.

"Let me peek in on Mrs. Blankenship and make sure things are okay."

"Mrs. Blankenship as in…"

He nodded. "Now you see why she might be upset."

Merriam Blankenship was beautiful in an elfin way, with high cheekbones and delicate features. She was one of the top-paid actors in the States, from what Sasha understood. "I'll wait here."

"I'll be out as soon as I can."

"No, take your time."

Nate went down a couple of doors, then with a quick knock he went inside. The sounds of crying intensified when the door opened, but muted again as soon as it swung shut. The soundproofing was obviously better here than at Saint Victoria Hospital. Then again, she couldn't remember ever getting a patient like this one.

She could see how Nate might have to perform a balancing act that she didn't have to deal with in the ER. Sure the island had its own wealthy population, but it wasn't on the scale that one found in other places in the world.

Nate stuck his head out. "Sasha, could you come in here please?"

That surprised her. But she braced herself to treat the woman like any other patient as she went into the room.

Merriam Blankenship's tear-stained face met her, lids swollen and her lashes plastered together.

"Merriam, this is Dr. James from our sister hospital in Williamtown. I just want her to have a look at you."

She wasn't a specialist in oncology or plastic surgery, so she wasn't sure exactly what Nate wanted to do, but there was a reason he'd called her in here. She just didn't want to mess it up. There were three other medical personnel in the room and a man who sat holding the woman's other hand. He must be her husband.

Moving toward the woman, she was surprised when Merriam reached her hand toward her. Sasha didn't stop to put gloves on; she knew there was healing in skin-to-skin touch that you couldn't get in other ways. She would glove up and sanitize her hands before she examined her.

"Do I look horrid?" Merriam turned to

look at her fully, revealing the cause of her distress. There was a large hole in the woman's cheek, some of the packing still wedged in it. According to what Nate had told her earlier, part of the cheekbone had to be removed.

Still, the question shocked her. Beneath Merriam's tears, Sasha could see real fear in her eyes. For someone who was used to looking gorgeous and idolized by millions, this would be a very hard blow. "No. Of course you don't." There was a stool next to the examination table where Merriam sat. Sasha sank down to be near her. "It looks like it does now because of the swelling and bruising. But Dr. Edwards only has the best of the best here at the hospital. I've seen wounds much, much worse than this have a good final result."

"Will I...look like me?"

She glanced up and Nate nodded to another man in the room, before he spoke up. "Dr. Seldridge has some renderings drawn up. Do you think you can look at them right now?"

Merriam's fingers went to Sasha's cheek, and she held very still to let her explore. "You're beautiful. You could be an actress too."

Sasha smiled. "No, I'm afraid I couldn't. My real feelings show far too easily. I'm not good at pretending to be someone I'm not. You have a rare gift."

"Thank you." She glanced at Nate and then Dr. Seldridge. "I'll look at what you have."

Sasha gave Merriam's hand a squeeze and got up to give the other doctor room to sit with his tablet. They went through the stages of the reconstruction process and Sasha was seriously impressed. This man had done his homework.

Then again, he would have. Nate would have made sure of it.

"How long?"

"Total, including healing time? Probably six months to a year."

Merriam glanced at her husband and whispered, "Can you check on when *Marriage of the Swans* is set to start filming?"

The man took out a device and scrolled through what looked like a calendar. "Nine months."

She blinked. "Will most of the work be done by then?"

"I can't promise, but I imagine so, but there may still be some redness from scarring."

"Makeup will cover scarring as long as the skin is smooth." She seemed to muse to herself. "It's not my best side and I can ask filming to take that into consideration."

Her husband smiled. "See? Not a tragedy."

"You got clean margins?"

"Yes. We'll want to scan you to make sure nothing lights up, but we're optimistic it hasn't spread."

"Thank God." She nodded. "Okay. Let's get this show on the road. I have a schedule to meet."

And for the first time since she'd come into the room, Merriam smiled and reached out to hug her husband. His whispered words reached her ears. "You're always the most beautiful woman in the room."

Sasha wasn't offended. Because the words were said in love. Merriam could be disfigured for life, and she was positive the words her husband uttered would have been exactly the same as they were now. She couldn't imagine being loved like that. Except for by her mom.

Her gaze went to Nate and found him looking at her. She quickly averted her eyes to the wall behind him hoping he just saw it as a passing glance that meant nothing.

Because it did. It meant nothing.

Three minutes later, they were on their way down the hallway. "Thanks for coming in. I just felt that if a woman she'd never seen before could come in and not flinch or recoil, it would help her feel better."

"It kind of helps that I'm a surgeon and an ER doc and have seen almost everything."

He laughed. "Yes, it does. But you're also compassionate. And that came through in droves."

"I'm glad."

The emergency had broken the ice and made meeting him here a little easier. Except for his reaction to her question about the clinic having an obstetrics department. She could see how that might have sent him into a panic.

"Hey. I just want you to know that even if I had somehow wound up pregnant—which I don't see happening—I wouldn't expect anything out of you. I don't believe in partnering with someone for reasons other than love."

"Sometimes you don't have a choice."

"There's always a choice."

He didn't say anything, just quickened his step enough that she had to hurry to keep up. He realized almost immediately and slowed back down with an apology. Something she'd said had struck a nerve. Had he found himself in exactly that situation at one point and been forced to provide support?

But he'd said he didn't have children. Unless someone had manipulated a situation or lied.

Although she wasn't going to ask him, if he didn't want to talk about it. She decided to make small talk instead. "So you know about my dad and have met my mom. What do your parents think of you starting your own clinic?"

He stopped and turned toward her. "What made you ask that?"

"No reason, really. I was just curious. They must be proud of you."

"Not so much." He took off walking again. "Our first patient is just ahead."

And that subject was evidently *entèdi*, as well. Fine.

But why on earth would he think his parents wouldn't be proud of him? He had accomplished so much.

As much as his response stung, she found her heart aching for him. What child didn't seek the approval of his mom and dad? Her father, even though he'd died far too young, had been proud of her accomplishments and had never been shy about telling her.

"So who is this next patient?"

He paused outside a door. "A forty-five-year-old man who was just diagnosed with amyloidosis."

"That's young, isn't it, for that kind of diagnosis? Is it someone from Saint Victoria?"

"Yes. He'd been complaining of gastrointestinal issues for a while. They thought it was IBS, but then some other symptoms came up. Swollen tongue, etc. They referred him here from Saint Victoria Hospital three weeks ago. Testing shows the ATTR form."

Meaning it was the hereditary form of the condition.

Amyloidosis was a devastating, incurable disease. It was also rare. She hadn't run into a case of it during her entire career. At least not that she knew of. It was also notoriously hard to diagnose, so like with this patient, it was often mistaken for other conditions.

"Is his heart affected? Lungs?"

"No, not yet. It's still early enough that we have some treatment options. His hematologist will be in a little later today."

Nate pushed the door open, and she followed him in. She put on her professional smile and glanced at the patient. She blinked. Blinked again. Her smile faded.

"Sasha, *nyès*, what are you doing here?" the patient asked.

Nate's glance went from one to the other. "You two know each other?"

Bondye, this couldn't be happening. Tears welled up in her eyes, but she forced them back, running a thousand words over in her mind, but rejecting them all. Instead she asked, "Why did you not tell us?"

"I couldn't. Not yet, anyway. Plus, I did not want to alarm anyone."

Too late. She was officially alarmed.

She looked at Nate and nodded. "This is Art James. Art is my uncle."

CHAPTER EIGHT

Art James was Sasha's uncle?

Hell, he should have realized the second he heard the last name.

Sasha sank onto the stool beside the man, just like she had when talking to Merriam Blankenship. But there were none of the smiles or compassion. There was just confusion.

"How could you not tell us you were coming here for tests? We had no idea. At least Mom never mentioned it."

"I didn't tell her. I wanted to see if treatment worked. If it does, it will buy me more time. Years maybe."

She swallowed. "You shouldn't be going through this alone."

Art had said he wasn't married and had no children. He'd made it sound like he didn't have any close relatives at all, which was another reason the name didn't click. Then again, Nate and his parents weren't close, so maybe they were estranged. But Sasha didn't act like they were.

"I don't want your mother to know. Not yet. She's been through enough. But I would have had to tell you. They said this form can be inherited. In a gene. Maybe your dad—"

"Let's worry about that later. Right now, I want to concentrate on you." She turned to Nate. "When does he start treatment?"

Art answered. "I do an infusion tomorrow. They said they want to knock this thing back on its ass." He grinned. "Well, they didn't quite use that language."

"I imagine they didn't."

Nate smiled. "We're going to use melphalan and dexamethasone. Hopefully we can achieve remission, and he'll start to feel better."

There was no cure for amyloidosis, but if they could slow the rate that amyloids were deposited in the tissues, the body could heal some of the damage done. Patients sometimes lived fairly normal lives for years to come.

"That's why I'm here, today. To make sure everything looks good for the infusion tomorrow."

Nate leaned closer to Art. "Now that she's

here, can I share what we're looking at? I'm pretty sure she'll want to know. And there's no more hiding it at this point, since you can't make yourself invisible."

"Are you sure about that?" Art chuckled, then got serious again. "Tell her what you told me about the gene test we did. About the fifty percent chance."

"Let's deal with you, first." He softened his response with a smile.

Normally they worried about the inherited form of amyloidosis in children of the patient. But Art had no children. Although Sasha had also said her dad died of a heart attack. Due to undiagnosed amyloidosis?

Hell. He hoped not. His chest contracted at the thought. But he needed to concentrate on this patient right now. They could deal with those other questions later.

Nate sat down with them and went over the particulars. What he could expect from treatment. Some of the side effects he might face from the chemo drug.

"How long will he be here?"

Sasha's question wasn't unexpected, but there wasn't a simple answer. "We'll want to keep him overnight after his infusion so we can monitor his immediate reaction to it. Then we'll send him home."

Sasha looked at Art. "I'll come and check in on you at home, the first couple of nights. Do you want me to stay with you?"

Art shook his head. "No. I'll be fine. I'm a pretty tough old goat."

"I know that for a fact." She smiled. "We will need to discuss when and where we tell my mom though."

At this, her uncle's chin jutted out just a bit. "We can discuss it, but no promises."

"It's a deal." She got up and hugged him, kissing the top of his head. "I love you, Uncle Art. I'll be here for your infusion."

Art frowned. "You don't have to work?"

"I'm actually off this week, so I asked to put in some hours here at The Island Clinic."

"Are you sure you want to spend it sitting with me?" asked Art.

"I'm positive."

Once they left the room, Sasha turned to Nate. "My dad was almost fifteen years older than his brother. Everyone assumed he'd just had a heart attack. Is it possible..."

He knew what she was thinking. If her dad had amyloidosis and they'd found it, maybe he could have been treated.

"Do you want to take a genetic test, just to rule out that you inherited it?"

"I do. Just so I'll know the risks of having

children. And what I might be facing some-day." There was a frown that said she really was worried.

He reached out and squeezed her hand. "Hey, he's not your father, so the chances of you having the markers might not be as high."

"No, but I just have this gut feeling, Nate. I think my dad had it. And just didn't know it. My mom is going to be asking the same questions. If my test comes back negative, it'll take one worry off her."

She could very well be right. And he didn't agree with Art about keeping this from his family.

Maybe it was because his parents had kept their plans from him until it was almost too late. So when they did finally tell him, the damage had been done and trust was broken. Hopefully it hadn't quite gotten to that point with Art, Tessi and Sasha.

And if Sasha had inherited the gene?

Something in his gut rebelled against that thought. But the only way they would know was if they pulled her blood and sent it in.

And if he hadn't worn a condom in the water? If she'd gotten pregnant? Damn.

"So you want to be tested? You're sure?"

"I am. Can you pull the blood?"

"I can, but we have phlebotomists who are very good, if you want me to call one."

She shook her head. "I'd rather you do it, if that's okay. The sooner the better. It's just the shock of seeing him in that room. I never suspected…"

"I know. And if I had realized exactly who he was, I wouldn't have taken you in there."

She stopped and looked at him. "So if you had known that Art was my uncle and that he had an inherited form of amyloidosis, you would have kept it from me?"

Would he have? What if Art had chosen never to tell any of his family and Sasha went through her life without knowing and developed it. When it was too late to do anything about it?

"Ethically, I should say yes."

"And if I had a child who later developed it?"

"I said ethically. What I would have probably done was talk to Art and try to convince him that you deserved to know, the same as if he'd had Huntington's or any other of the familial conditions."

"Okay. I can handle that. I'd like to think my uncle would have eventually decided to do the right thing." She touched his arm. "He's a good man."

"I know. I've sat and talked to him for a bit. I think he was telling the truth. He wanted to wait and see what form he had." He paused. "I'll take you to my office, and then I'll retrieve the items needed to do the blood draw."

"Will he be okay alone?"

"The hematologist will be there in a minute. And I'll check in on him, as well."

He unlocked his office door and ushered her inside. "Have a seat wherever you'll be most comfortable, and I'll be back in a minute."

Sasha wandered around Nate's office for a minute or two, not really seeing anything. Had her father had amyloidosis? It was surreal that he could have died from something that had been eating away at his system for years. But then the early signs tended to be vague, and her dad had always been pretty stoic about his health. By the time of his heart attack, though, he had to have been feeling bad. And yet he'd said nothing.

"Why, Papi? You could have been here with us longer."

But it wasn't his fault. He hadn't known what he had, or he would have tried to get treatment. She caught sight of the doll on Nate's shelf. Her dad wasn't to blame, just as that child's parents weren't to blame for her death. They couldn't have known. And Sasha's dad didn't know, of that she could be sure.

That helped a little. She had no idea how her mom was going to react. But Sasha felt strongly that she needed to know. And it wasn't up to her to make decisions for other people.

And if she had it? God, she could kind of understand why Art might hesitate to let her mom know. He'd want to save her the worry. Sasha could see herself wanting to do the same. But that wasn't fair to her mother.

And what about kids? Did that mean she'd never hold a baby in her arms? Her chest tightened until it was hard to breathe. And marriage? Could she see putting her husband through the pain of watching her slowly waste away if she developed a severe form of the condition?

She went to the couch and sank into the deep leather cushions. They smelled clean and masculine. Like Nate's scent when he'd held her on that beach. She breathed deeply, allowing it to calm her spirit, to bring her back from the panic that had welled inside her. As a surgeon, she knew that treatments for amyloidosis had drastically improved. It couldn't be cured, but it could be managed. Sometimes for a relatively long period of time.

She sighed. Why couldn't things be simple? Like Nate's lingering scent that clung to his couch. But they weren't. And neither was Nate.

Even by virtue of his offer to go and get the supplies needed to draw her blood. Not just anyone could take it on themselves to do that. Only someone with clout…or money, could bypass the normal protocol of things like that. She'd seen that in Austin in a lot of little ways. When he went to a professor to ask something, that professor almost always made himself available. It had impressed her at first. But then she started to question the way it reinforced feelings of entitlement and being above the rules that others had to follow. And the way Austin could just move to New York with never a thought as to what it would do to Sasha. He'd just done it because…he could. Because he took it for granted that he could always find someone else.

And yet, in asking Nate to draw her blood, wasn't she falling into the same trap? Using her familiarity with him to gain a favor? So wasn't she just as guilty?

Probably. And it made her slightly nauseous. She didn't want to take advantage or use people for what she could get from them.

He came back in with a carry tray and a couple of vials, before she could go very far down that avenue of thought. "You're sure."

Now would be the time to say she'd made a mistake and ask him to please call one of the phlebotomists. Or say that she didn't want to be tested. But she didn't. Instead, she nodded.

Then he slowly knelt in front of her and took her hand in his.

She swallowed. Would she ever have children? Would someone kneel in front of her like this and ask her to marry him, if it turned out she'd inherited the condition? Would they even want to, knowing the possibilities? Damn! She needed to get a hold of herself. All of this speculating was doing her no good.

"Which arm?"

"Right one." He wasn't proposing to her. Nor would he ever. And she didn't want him to.

"Make a fist."

She stretched out her arm, watching as he pulled a piece of rubber strapping tight around her upper arm. He tapped the crook of her elbow, looking for a likely vein. Then he slid the needle home, getting the right spot on the very first try. Clicking a vial onto the end, he let the suction pull blood into the container.

"Release your fist." When the first vial was full, he popped it off and put the second one on. And yes, he definitely smelled like his couch.

The vials were already labeled with her name. "What's your date of birth?"

She told him and he printed it on the sides of both tubes of blood. "I'll take these down to the lab, so they can send them off."

"How long will it take?"

"Two to four weeks. I'll put a rush on it."

She gripped his wrist. "No, don't. Please. Just send it off as you would anyone else's blood."

His head cocked as he looked at her, but he nodded. "Okay, but we ask for lab tests to be rushed all the time."

It reminded her of when he'd offered to have the helicopter pick her up at Saint Victoria Hospital. Her answer was just the same now as it was then. "I'd rather save that option for the people who really need it."

Maybe he remembered that incident too, because he gave a slight shrug and climbed to his feet and left the room, taking the tote with him.

Two to four weeks and she would know if she was likely to develop amyloidosis. She almost wished she'd opted to remain in the dark. But that would be unethical, especially if she met someone someday who actually wanted to have children with her. It was an autosomal-dominant trait, so all that was needed was one copy of the gene to pass it on. Her copy. So her children would have a 50 percent chance of inheriting the mutated gene. The odds were bad enough that she might not risk having children if she was a carrier of the trait. Unless she was willing to take a prenatal test and consider terminating the pregnancy if the fetus carried the gene. The thought of making a decision like that...

Maybe she should tell him to forget about sending her blood off until later, when her emotions had settled down.

But it was too late for that. Besides, she'd rather know now...start treatment early.

He was back in a minute or two, sans the blood kit. "Thank you for doing that for me. I probably shouldn't have asked."

"Yes, you should have. And I know it's a shock. But there's a good chance you don't have the gene."

"If my dad had it, there's a good chance that I do."

He sat down beside her. "Let's just wait and see what the findings are."

"Okay." She forced herself to shake off the sense of melancholy that had enveloped her. "Are there other patients to see?"

"I had someone else take over rounds this morning."

Something else he had the option of doing because of his position. And yet, again, it was because of her. "I'm sorry. I've disrupted your whole routine. I think I should go."

"You haven't disrupted anything. I normally do rounds just because I feel a duty to the clinic to follow up on its patients."

That made sense.

He went on. "Your uncle never married."

"No. He was engaged once, but it didn't work out. Her parents had very high standards and didn't think he was good enough for her. And even though she didn't agree with that assessment, they succeeded in putting a wedge between them. They were embarrassed that their daughter might marry someone from a poorer background. Can you imagine a parent acting like that? Shouldn't they have wanted her to be…happy?"

When she glanced up at him, she saw that

a muscle was working in his jaw. Surely he didn't agree with Corinne's parents. "My uncle actually did very well for himself. I think maybe their contempt spurred him to work extra hard just to show them what he was made of."

"And did it work? Were they at least sorry for coming between them?"

"I don't know. He and Corinne were broken up by that time, so it didn't really matter. It was kind of ironic, because as far as I know she never married either."

"They never got back together?"

"She broke my uncle's heart. I think he found it hard to trust anyone after that. He poured himself into his job, instead."

He muttered something she didn't catch. "Sorry?"

"Nothing. Just I can understand that. You spend a large chunk of time thinking you know someone, only to find out you don't, when it really matters."

He could have been talking about her and Austin. Maybe he was, in fact. "I know what you mean."

"Your ex?"

"Yep. I think everyone must have an ex they can look back on like that."

"I think most of us can."

"You've had a serious relationship?"

One of his brows went up and he leaned back against the sofa. "It depends what you mean by serious. I've never been engaged, but I was dating someone I expected to someday marry."

She hadn't known that about him. What had happened to break them up?

"I wasn't engaged, either," she said, "but five years sure seemed serious, at the time."

"I would consider that a serious relationship too."

She sighed. "My mom always hoped to be a grandmother. I don't know if that will ever happen, now. Do yours feel the same?"

"Doubtful. My parents were always about looking young and healthy."

She remembered his attitude when she'd asked about his parents before and didn't want to push it. But the little glimpses he'd let her see of his parents didn't impress her. In fact they sounded just a little bit like Corinne's parents. Sasha doubted that she would have measured up to their expectations, either. Not that she needed to worry about that. Still she was curious.

"You said you doubted they were proud of you when I asked earlier. Have they ever come here?"

"No. I haven't seen them since I moved to Saint Victoria."

Wow, that shocked her. "I would think they would have wanted to come and see The Island Clinic, since you founded the place."

He laid his arm over the back of the couch. "I don't think they're really interested."

His parents weren't interested in what he'd accomplished? That was just strange. She knew they were wealthy, because the rumors were that Nate had started the clinic using the money from his trust fund. It had been a hefty amount. He'd had a helipad built for Saint Victoria Hospital, after all.

"If that's true, then I'm sorry."

"It's true. And don't be sorry. I'm doing what I want to do. That's all that's important to me, right now."

So his relationship with his folks didn't count as important? Sasha couldn't imagine being estranged from her family. But not all families were like hers. Some were like Corinne's, destroying their child's chance for happiness. And from what it looked like, they'd had no regrets about it.

Could Nate's folks really be that bad?

"I get it. I'm doing what I want to do, as well. What makes me happy. Fortunately I'm doing it with my mom's blessing." Her mind went back to her uncle. "So if the chemo treatment works, how long will he have? My uncle, I mean."

"I figured that's who you were talking about. It's hard to put a number on it. But if we achieve an early remission, he has a chance of living ten years, maybe more."

"That's longer than I thought." She relaxed in her seat a bit. She'd been thinking one or two years max, so to hear it could be longer was a relief.

Maybe she should call Corinne. How would Sasha feel if someone she'd cared deeply for had a terminal illness and no one told her?

Not very good.

And yet, should she interfere? She saw the woman periodically at the store and they smiled at each other, but neither of them mentioned Art. She figured it was their business. It still was. But she'd been hurt to find her uncle had kept his condition from his own family. Well, she could decide about that later.

First she had to tell her mom about it. Or rather, they did, since she'd promised Art she wouldn't say anything about it right now. And she needed to keep that promise. Art didn't need any added stress at the moment.

She found her mind drifting for some reason and came to with a start when she realized her head had fallen back against the backrest of the sofa. She must have drifted off. It must have been because of the late night she'd had at the hospital last night. She'd been called in unexpectedly and had worked until after one in the morning. "I'm sorry. I really should go."

"No." He stood. "Why don't you stay and take a little nap. You've had a shock. I have some work to do behind my desk, so you'll have complete quiet."

She should just get up and drive back to Williamtown, but she was totally exhausted, even though it wasn't even noon yet. She didn't want to nod off on the drive home. But how did she feel about Nate watching her sleep? Not as embarrassed as she might have been, if she were wide awake. "Are you sure?"

"Yep. Positive." He went over to a closet and retrieved a pillow and a light blanket, smiling when he noticed her glance. "I sometimes sleep in here if I get tied up for too long. Pop your shoes off."

He set the pillow on the end of the couch that was nearest his desk. Sasha did as he asked and toed off her shoes, leaving them beside the sofa. Then she lay down and stretched out her legs, immediately wishing she hadn't when his scent rose up from the pillow against her cheek. He had slept on this very pillow, his head cradled in its softness. But other than jump up and race out of here, she had no choice but to pretend she didn't notice.

Nate shook out the blanket and draped it over her. "Okay?"

She wasn't sure it was anymore, but she needed to do her best to pretend she was just fine. "Are you sure you don't mind? I worked later than I expected last night, but I still shouldn't be this tired."

"Like I said, it was probably the shock of seeing Art in that room. Just rest. And then maybe we can sit down and talk a little more about the gala."

"That sounds like a plan. And I want to check in on my uncle in a while anyway before I leave."

"Okay."

With that, Nate ducked out of sight and headed back to his desk. Somehow it was comforting to know he was not far away. Would be clicking away at his computer or something.

For the first time in a long time, she let

her muscles relax and snuggled deeper into the blanket—the one that also carried Nate's scent.

And she let herself drift away.

CHAPTER NINE

"I CALLED YOUR father for a consult. I hope you don't mind."

It took Nate's brain a second to compute the meaning of the words. A quick wave of anger rose inside him. Totally unjustified, but it foamed and frothed in the background anyway. He'd been thinking of seeing Sasha curled up on his couch a few days ago, and hadn't been able to erase the image from his skull. She'd been sweet and totally relaxed, one arm hanging off the cushions, the other one tucked under her head. And that snore…

Well, it wasn't exactly a snore. More like a tiny snuffle that periodically pulled his attention from his paperwork.

Not that it was ever fully on his work.

"I'm assuming this is in regard to Merriam Blankenship's upcoming reconstruction surgery."

A surgery Sasha was supposed to come

and watch tomorrow. It would be the last day she would be working at The Island Clinic.

Dr. Seldridge nodded. "I've been here since the day this place opened, and I feel in some ways that the newest procedures have passed me by. Ones I might have heard about if I'd stayed in the States."

"I've always told the staff to take some time off, if needed, to go explore new protocols or take a furlough."

"I don't think I've been here long enough to warrant that, but I sent over the pictures of the surgical site and—"

"You withheld the name and blocked out features of her face, I'm hoping?" He could see his parents deciding to somehow use this to further their own practice.

And how cynical was that? In days gone by he would never have even had such a thought. But now? He himself had been the target of them trying to expand their horizons. And when he hadn't cooperated? They'd cut him off. But he didn't want to tell Frank any of that. There was no need.

"Of course. They offered to come over and consult in person, but I turned them down, saying it was a sensitive case."

When Frank had first started that sentence, Nate had tensed so hard his jaw ached. How he'd longed for his parents to come and visit his clinic. At first. Until it was obvious they were simply not interested. Or they were angry. But three years was a long time to harbor that kind of grudge.

He knew from experience. Because he'd done the exact same thing.

"I think you made the right call. Mrs. Blankenship came over here for the exact reason that she didn't want anyone to know about the surgery."

"I did get her permission to ask Jackson… your father."

Nate smiled. "I know who he is. And thank you for getting permission."

"I really want her to have a good outcome." Frank dropped into one of the chairs flanking Nate's desk.

"I do, as well. Was the call able to reassure you?"

"Yes. Your dad said he would take the exact multipronged approach that I planned to. He seemed very interested in what we do here."

He decided to ignore that last sentence. "I never had any doubt that your approach was the right one. It's why I worked so hard to bring you here." As uncomfortable as it made him to know that his father had probably heard Nate's name mentioned in conversation, he couldn't fault Frank for calling him. In his place he might have done the same. He held not only a person's looks, but their livelihood in his hands. And while it was true, you couldn't always work miracles, plastic surgery was one of those specialties where people seemed to expect just that. He'd heard that time and time again from his parents. It was part of what had turned him off to going into plastic surgery. Their conversations about who had done what, or who had done a terrible job on someone's face or body had rubbed him the wrong way. The emphasis wasn't on the quality of life, or helping people, but about outdoing their fellow surgeons.

Nate had interviewed his prospective staff members carefully, for just that reason. He did not want that kind of competitive spirit at The Island Clinic. He wanted the focus to be wholly on helping their patients and supporting Saint Victoria Hospital.

He hoped even Sasha was beginning to see that. Everything about his clinic was geared toward that, from the huge bronze statue of a little girl out front, her hands outstretched with a sign at her feet promising We Are Always Here to Help, to the clinic's five-star restaurant that not only fed the rich and famous, but also provided free meals to family members of patients who couldn't afford to pay.

Frank had definitely fit the profile of what the clinic looked for in a doctor. Even his calling Nate's dad bore evidence of that. He wanted a good outcome…for the patient, not for himself. *That* was why he had called Jackson Edwards.

"So you're not upset I called him? I felt like I needed to tell you."

"I'm not upset." It was true. He'd been pretty angry when he first realized what Frank had done, but now that he'd had time to really think it through, he agreed with the decision. Hadn't Nate even thought about calling his parents to do the exact same thing Frank had? And if he had, he wouldn't have blamed Frank for being upset at him for going around him, since Frank was the specialist.

And he was very glad his parents weren't coming to Saint Victoria. As he'd watched Sasha sleeping on his couch, for a split second he wondered what it might be like to have a life like other people had. To be able to love and be loved and not wonder if there was some kind of motive underlying those expressions of love.

And who would this mythical person be?

Sasha's face flashed across his mind's eye.

No. Frank's confession just brought home all the reasons why he didn't trust love. Didn't trust his own ability to read people. Because he'd been so very wrong about his parents. One thing he hadn't been wrong about, though, was moving to this island. This felt more like home than anywhere he'd ever been. Even when Sasha had looked at him with suspicion that first day. Because it just made him want to show her and anyone else that his motivation wasn't to puff himself up and make himself look important. He didn't care how he looked. He just wanted to do good.

"Everything still a go for the surgery tomorrow? Mrs. Blankenship is more optimistic?"

"I don't think that I would use the word *optimistic*. But she's no longer in a state of panic. She knows that if she left the tumor, it would eventually spread farther and kill her. I think her husband convinced her that all he cared about was having her with him."

Nate's chest tightened. He'd never experienced that type of love. Not from his parents. Not from Tara or any other woman.

"Good." Nate glanced at the other doctor. "I have Sasha James coming to observe tomorrow, is that okay?"

"She's the one who came in and calmed Merriam down?"

"Yes. I wanted her to see how we do surgery here at The Island Clinic." He smiled, remembering the day he met her. "When I first met her, she was a little less than impressed by what she thought we were doing here."

"Why?"

The question was fair, but Nate could see the other side of it. With wealthy people flying in and off the island for quiet, private procedures, it could seem like they were using the island just for privacy and to make money. He believed she was changing her mind. At least he hoped she was. He wasn't sure why it mattered so much to him, but it did.

Because they'd had sex? Maybe. But it was more than that, although he didn't really want to examine it too closely.

"I think some people might see the Merriam Blankenships sliding in and out of the hospital and think this is just a money-making operation."

"Really? I think that statue out front makes it pretty plain that's not the case."

"She'd never even visited the clinic up until a couple of weeks ago. I'm hoping the gala will bring more people in to see what we're about—what we're *really* about."

There was a little part of him that hoped maybe Sasha's mom was going to rub a bit of the gilt off the trappings and make The Island Clinic a little more…homey? Was that the right word? Not quite. Maybe *inviting*.

He hoped Sasha herself would be able to convince those who still thought they were here for nefarious reasons that it wasn't that at all. Nothing was more convincing than a person who had herself been convinced.

At least he hoped that was true. And with Sasha's mom and her "small army" of local vendors heading things up, this fund-raiser would be even more spectacular than if they served truffles on alabaster plates.

As if he'd read Nate's mind, Frank said, "I think you're doing the right thing having this catered locally."

He'd been hearing that from person after person. "I'm hoping everyone else sees that as a good thing, as well."

Frank paused. "Speaking of Dr. James. Is she involved, do you know?"

"In the gala preparations?"

The surgeon shook his head. "No, I'm talking more in terms of romantic involvement."

Nate's mind froze in place for several seconds. When he could think again, the word *yes* hung on his lips only to be swallowed back. She wasn't involved.

He knew that how? Because she'd slept with him? Because she'd had a terrible experience with that Austin person?

She wouldn't have a bad experience with Frank though. He was sure of that. The plastic surgeon was a good man.

But damn, Nate did not want him to ask her out. At all. Someone was bound to at some point, but at least if that happened, he probably wouldn't know who it was. Would just hear about it in some roundabout fashion. Wouldn't have to watch Sasha come over to The Island Clinic and…kiss someone.

"I really don't know. You'll have to ask her that question."

"Maybe I will. Just thought I'd ask and see if you knew anything."

Nate could always tell him he'd had wild

sex with her just down the beach from the hospital. But he was pretty sure Sasha would kill him if he breathed a word of that encounter to anyone.

So why didn't he want her dating Frank?

He had no idea. But the faster he got the other doctor out of his office, the better. Because the last thing he wanted to talk about with another man was Sasha James.

Nate dropped into the seat beside her.

Sasha's insides knotted the second she saw him. She was a little surprised that he'd opted to observe the surgery with her. Surely he had more important things to do than to babysit her. But who said he was there to do that?

She'd been at the clinic on and off over the last week, but had barely seen Nate since she'd fallen asleep on his couch. She'd come to sit with her uncle when he'd had his infusion, but Nate hadn't appeared that day, either. She'd wondered if he was avoiding her, in fact. And yet here he was suddenly appearing at Merriam's surgery.

Well, this was a high-profile case. It probably had nothing to do with her at all. He probably had to be there for the ones who could line the clinic's pockets. She immediately pulled herself up for the thought. Because the clinic was supporting Saint Victoria Hospital in a very real way. It was why her uncle was able to receive his treatments, probably at minimal or no cost.

"Are they running late?" she asked.

The patient wasn't in the room yet, but this was the time that Nate had given her when he last saw her. Actually that was the morning she'd slept in his office after being floored by her uncle's presence at the hospital.

And looking back, she couldn't understand why she'd let herself do that. If it had been any other doctor at this hospital or at hers, she wouldn't have. Would have forced herself to wake up and get a grip on her emotions. Was she letting her guard down around Nate without realizing it?

Oh, she hoped not.

"Yes, a few minutes. Frank wanted to go over the procedure with Merriam and her husband one last time before she went under sedation."

"I can't blame him. Any patient would be lucky to have him. He's incredibly thorough."

Nate stiffened beside her. "Yes. He is."

There was something about the way he

said that, almost as if there was something wrong with that observation. But what?

"I don't know him personally, but he's a very good doctor, from what you've said."

He settled back in his chair again. What on earth?

"He's got a good plan for this patient."

Just then the doors opened and in came a gurney. It was wheeled over to where the surgical team was assembling. Various people spoke to the patient who nodded, then a nurse moved to set up the drips.

"Will Frank be in before she's under?"

"You seem to have gotten the hang of calling everyone by their first names. Even those you don't know very well."

Touché. But then again, she hadn't liked Nate very much when he'd first asked her to use his.

And now? She swallowed. Well, now she might like him just a little too much. That, in and of itself, should send alarm bells pealing in her head. But there was nothing in there but the periodic chirp of a cricket. And a low hum of awareness.

This man had seen her at her most vulnerable. She should be a ball of nerves even sitting beside him. Instead, along with awareness, there was this subtle undercurrent of excitement. Anticipation. A woozy sense of euphoria, even.

But why? If she was hoping to repeat that scene in the ocean, she could forget it. That was not happening. They'd both made that promise. And yet this man had a way of getting under her skin and making her do unexpected things.

Just like Austin had?

She hoped not. That had been a huge disaster. This might even be a bigger one, seeing as they had to work together. Seeing as her mother was almost heading up his gala single-handedly. And seeing as she might have the gene for amyloidosis.

Her heart squeezed in her chest. Sasha needed to be careful. More than careful. If not, she could mess this up for a lot of people, including her mom. Including herself.

"Well, you kind of insisted I call you by your first name. I just assumed that went for everyone that worked here."

"You're right. It does."

But there was still something in his tone that worried her. "Is something wrong?"

"No, nothing." He nodded at the scene in front of them, where Frank had just come into the room. "There he is now."

Within minutes the patient was under general anesthesia, and they had a couple of work drapes set up. One at Merriam's hip area and one at her cheek. "Will he do the bone graft first?"

"Yes, he'll kind of have to, since he needs to set up the scaffolding on which to rebuild her cheek. They'll take a sliver of bone from her hip and set it in place. The bone should build density as it heals. Then they'll add muscle and a layer of fat tissue. Finally, they'll harvest skin from the same area they're taking the bone from, since the skin there is often a similar texture to what is on the face. They'll turn it into a mesh that they'll lay in place." He glanced at her. "There will be several revision surgeries to minimize any scarring and make sure the tissue is covering the way it should. There are always cheek implants that can help with that, as well."

Sasha was a surgeon, so knew a lot of the mechanics, but this was microsurgery. There were nerves and fine work that she didn't need to worry about. Yes, she tried to be aware of scarring when she stitched someone up, but her first concern was function. Aesthetics came second to that. And if it was something delicate, like a lip margin that had been sliced through, she normally called in a plastic surgeon just to make sure things were lined up the way they should be.

A shiver went over her. If only people worked like that. If only they could be lined up so they matched perfectly, so that just the right couples found each other. But that wasn't how things were in the real world. Relationships were messy and ugly and sometimes they were treacherous. And sometimes you never found the right person with whom to share your life. Or circumstances prevented it from becoming a reality.

Except... She was very aware of Nate beside her. Aware of his breathing, his movements, his posture. He was now leaning forward, elbows planted on his knees, fingers steepled as he watched what was happening below.

There was no doubt the man was gorgeous—he probably had women swarming around him. He had good looks and far too much charisma. And his physical features were put together in just the right way.

Ha! Kind of like what Frank was trying to accomplish in the surgery happening below.

And the way Nate made love...

Her eyes closed for a second as a wave of remembered sensation went over her. The water on her body, his warm hands stroking over her.

She sucked down a quick breath and sat up as emotions from that day threatened to pull her under.

"Everything okay?"

God, no, it wasn't. But she didn't know how to turn off the scenes playing in her head.

"Yes, fine." She stared straight ahead. "W-what's he doing now?"

"He's remodeling the remainder of bone in the cheek so he can fit what he's harvested in there."

She knew what the surgeon was doing, but it was the only thing she could think of to say that would force back the tide in her skull. Did Nate ever think about that day? Or had he been able to just sweep it away and forget about those tiny moments that went into what had happened between them?

Moments like laughing at the wave that had swept over them on the beach. Moments like handing her the paper bag that held her underwear.

Oh, what a mess she'd made by having sex with him.

And there was no way to undo it. Just like there'd been no way to undo what had happened with Austin.

All she could do was push through it and move on to the next chapter of her life.

Except all those chapters contained Nate in some way, shape or form, unless he decided to leave his position at The Island Clinic. And she didn't see that happening. He loved it here.

So she forced her attention back down to what was happening in the room beneath them. Frank was moving from one step to another, his hands steady. She couldn't see his face, but she imagined it was just as calm and methodical as his fingers.

If only Sasha could be the same. Maybe she could though. She could move through these next days, these next months with methodical deliberation. She would walk with her uncle through his treatments, wait on her own diagnosis. And do her best to enjoy life. Enjoy her job. Even enjoy these moments next to Nate. Because life sped on by no matter what came your way. You couldn't go back and redo any of it.

So make the best of it.

And if she made the mistake of sleeping with Nate again?

Well, mistake or not, life would move on down the road, right? She wouldn't be stuck in those moments forever. So she should enjoy them while she could.

Nate's phone buzzed. He glanced down at the readout and frowned. Dragged a hand through his hair. When he looked her way, Sasha was careful to act like her attention had been on the surgery below.

"I need to go outside and deal with this. I should be back soon."

"Okay."

If it was anything to do with her uncle he would have told her, right? So apart from that, it was none of her business who was calling him. Probably something about the gala.

Or maybe it was a woman. Someone else he'd been with.

He left the room and Sasha forced her mind off the disturbing thought of Nate having a girlfriend and back toward what was happening below. She could hear Frank's voice as he called out for instruments or spoke a summary that would mark part of the official transcripts of the surgery. From what she could make out, all was going according to plan.

Nate was back within five minutes. The frown was still there.

"Is everything okay?"

He dropped back into his seat. "I'm not sure."

How could you not be sure everything was okay? "Anything I can help with?"

"Not unless you know of a magical way to deal with relatives."

She forced her eyes to go wide. "You have met my mom, right?"

"I'd take a thousand of your moms over dealing with my parents."

His parents! Not some woman waiting in the wings.

Nate had said his parents had never visited the clinic. Had all but said that they weren't proud of what he'd done. "Was that them on the phone?"

"Yes, Frank mentioned he'd called my father to consult with him on Merriam's surgery."

That surprised her. "I thought they weren't interested in The Island Clinic?"

"They're not. Unless they can get something out of it."

He made them sound pretty awful. "Was the phone call about the surgery?"

"Actually no. It was about the gala. They've decided to come to it. Out of the blue."

Maybe people could change.

"That's great." She looked at his face and reconsidered. "Isn't it?"

"I'm not sure." He rubbed his palm down his face. "I don't know what their angle is yet."

"Maybe there's not one. Maybe they realized they needed to make amends."

"I don't think that's even possible at this point. There's too much water under that particular bridge."

"But why? Do you want to talk about it?"

He stared straight ahead for several long moments. Either he hadn't heard the question, or he'd decided to ignore it. So she pretended she'd never posed the question.

Then Nate turned toward her. "Actually, I think I would. Do you want to grab a coffee, or would you rather stay here until the surgery is completed?"

She glanced down where the operation was still going strong. "I think they're going to be there for a while." Frank was still working on the bone graft. She imagined this could take close to eight or ten hours. "So we can go and always come back if there's time."

There was a relief on Nate's face she'd never seen there before. All of a sudden, she was glad she was there. Glad he was willing to confide in her—or at least tell her about whatever was bothering him.

They stood and Nate opened the door for her, and together they headed down the hallway toward the cafeteria.

CHAPTER TEN

NATE WASN'T SURE why he'd told Sasha he wanted to talk about his parents, but he did want to. Maybe because she was from Saint Victoria Hospital and he wouldn't have to face her day in and day out, like he would Frank or his other colleagues. Or maybe it was because she'd shared stuff about herself that he was pretty sure not everyone knew.

They went into the coffee shop and found a quiet corner and sat down. "What would you like?"

"A cappuccino, if they have it."

"They do."

Her brows went up. "I figured they did."

He thought there might be an undercurrent there, but if there was, she was hiding it pretty well. Maybe she was just being polite back in the observation room. He couldn't imagine anything worse than seeing her eyes glaze in boredom as he spilled out the sordid details of the rift between him and his parents. "Listen, don't feel like you have to sit here and listen to—"

"I'm the one who offered." She laid her hand on his arm. "Go get our coffees. I'll be here when you get back."

He turned to go, the words she'd just said sliding over him. *I'll be here when you get back.*

Did she know how that sounded? Whether she did or not, he wasn't prepared for the wave of emotion that washed over him at the words. He went up and stood in line, mulling over what it would be like for someone like Sasha to be there for you, no matter what. To never have to wonder if she was telling the truth. To never have to wonder if she was sizing up what you could do for her.

To just be there…for you.

He liked it. Liked the idea of someone being there when you got home. Of someone being there to hear about your day and to tell you about theirs.

But unfortunately that wasn't in the cards for him.

Or was it?

He glanced back at where Sasha sat, and found her watching him, her beautiful face soft and accessible.

Hell. What if that "someone" was… Sasha?

His mind went to hell all of a sudden, various parts of his brain going to war with the other parts. Maybe it was just the fact that she was willing to listen. Once he told her about his parents, he would likely change the dynamic between them. Did he want her to feel sorry for him? Hell no. That was the last thing he wanted.

So he would just tell her and go from there.

He ordered their coffees and when they were ready he threw some packets of sugar and sweetener on the tray before carrying it back to the table. "I wasn't sure what you took in yours."

Picking up two of the yellow packets, she ripped them open and hesitated as she looked at her coffee. "I always hate messing up the pictures they draw with the frothed milk."

There was a heart with what looked like an arrow going through it. He stiffened. Had the barista done it on purpose? Nate had had coffee in here with various other people, but he didn't think he'd ever brought anyone who was more than just a colleague in here.

"I'm sure they're used to it."

Sasha dumped the packets in. "I'm sure they are, but it still seems sad." She stirred, removing all traces of the image. Just as well, because he was starting to get some very strange thoughts going through his head.

He took a sip of his espresso, very glad there was no room for pictures or anything else in the tiny demitasse cup. Just solid black liquid. He glanced at her. "How is it?"

"Perfect." She smiled and propped her elbows on the edge of the table, her cup cradled between her hands. She was lithe and beautiful and her attention focused solely on him. "So. Tell me why you don't want your parents to come to the gala."

"I didn't say that."

"You didn't say it outright, but it was there in your body language. Or am I wrong."

Oh, she wasn't wrong. But it was a little disconcerting that she could read him so well. Could everyone else? He'd always considered himself a pretty tough nut to crack. The people who'd tried normally pulled back pretty quickly when they realized he wasn't interested in cozy little tête-à-têtes about his personal life. Stuff about the clinic? Fine, he welcomed that all day long. But his relationships were off-limits. To everyone.

Until now.

He had a decision to make. He could put a halt to this before the conversation began, or he could continue and accept whatever consequences it brought.

"You're not wrong," he said.

"But why? They're your parents."

"They are, but we haven't spoken in years. Since I came back from my tour with Medicine Around the World."

She took a sip of her coffee, licking off a tiny fleck of cream that stuck to her lip. His stomach twisted when her tongue darted back into her mouth. He remembered the slide of her tongue against his as they kissed in the sea.

"Was that after Hurricane Regan, when you came to Saint Victoria?"

"It was. I arrived home to a press release and a ribbon-cutting ceremony at my parents' clinic."

She blinked, and he couldn't blame her confusion.

"Before you ask, the problem wasn't the ribbon cutting. The problem was, I was expected to specialize in plastic surgery and join their practice. And they announced it without consulting me. There were photographers and reporters, and cameras were flashing and…"

"And you were in shock." She reached

across the table. "Oh, God. That was after Marie…"

"Yes. I found out what the diagnosis was just before boarding the flight. I had the doll in my hand."

A jumble of tangled emotions went through him as he remembered the horror of that sight. Of his parents' and Tara's wide smiles as they handed him a glass of champagne. One he took, still not understanding exactly what was happening. He set the doll on a table beside him, only to have his mom pick it up and look at it, an expression of utter disgust coming into her face, and make a nasty comment.

He'd taken the doll from her and set his glass on the table. As photographers continued to snap their pictures he turned to them and caught sight of the plaque on the wall.

No, he'd said. And he turned and walked away from the clinic, catching a cab and taking it back to his apartment.

"They evidently didn't take it well when you told them you were planning on coming back here instead of joining their practice."

He gave a rough laugh. "You could say that. They called me, accused me of being selfish and insensitive. Of embarrassing them in front of everyone. Said that if I went through with coming to Saint Victoria, I was no longer welcome in their home."

Her fingers squeezed his. "They actually said that?"

"Yep."

A look of anger came over her face. *"Modi. Paran ou yo se moun fou."*

He knew what that first word meant, but had no idea about the rest. "Translation, please?"

"You don't want to know." She gave him a smile. "Let's just say it wasn't very complimentary toward your mom and dad."

He laughed. Somehow her saying that put into words all the things he hadn't said during that terrible time. Even if he didn't quite understand it. "I probably made them sound worse than they were."

"Did they say those things?"

"Yes."

"Then no, they're even *worse* than you made them sound."

He sighed. "I think they were hurt. They'd built this up into a huge deal. And part of it was my fault. I never explicitly told them no. But when Marie died, I knew I wasn't going to be happy with just sitting in an office consulting with plastic surgery cases all day. I wanted to do more with my life than that.

Not that there's anything wrong with what my parents do. It just isn't for me. And what I'm doing isn't for them. My mom would hate living so close to the beach."

She took another sip of her coffee, watching him over the top of the cup. "And yet you don't hate the beach. Didn't you say you go out there a lot?"

"I do. It's one of my favorite spots in the world."

More so now, after what they'd done there. The only problem was, it was hard to go out there without seeing Sasha lying on that beach laughing, her clothing soaked, looking up at him with those dark eyes and even darker lashes. Of seeing her as she let go of him and lay back in the water.

His body reacted, just as it always did.

"It's one of my favorite spots in the world too."

He had a feeling she knew what he was thinking.

She set her cup down and looked at him. "What are you going to do about your mom and dad? Are you going to let them come?"

"I think so, yes. I don't need their approval, but I would like them to see why I couldn't join their practice."

"Do you think they'll understand?"

Unfortunately, he didn't think it would change a damned thing. But he somehow wanted them to acknowledge that there were other paths. Other ways to find fulfillment in life. "I don't know. Most of me doesn't think so, and part of me isn't exactly sure why they want to come."

Sasha's eyes softened. "Maybe they've realized that they misjudged you, Nate." She paused. "Just like I did."

His chest filled with some strange emotion that defied explanation. "You did?"

"I think so. I thought you were just some rich *monché* with a savior complex."

"Monché?"

"Dude…man…"

He laughed. "I don't think I have a savior complex, at least I hope I don't. I just want to help people, Sasha. Truly."

She gripped his hand. "I know that now. Truly." Her head tilted. "That statue in front of the clinic, is it…"

"Yes. It's Marie. I asked her parents if I could erect it there, and they gave me permission."

"I like that." She gave a visible swallow. "While her death should never have happened, I'm glad that we can now saves lives like hers."

He leaned closer and took both of her hands. "Thank you for that. I never really told anyone who that statue represented, and you're the first person to see the connection."

"I doubt I am. I'm just not as polite as other people. I tend to say what I think."

"That's one of the things I..." His mind switched tracks just in time. "That I like about you."

Her mouth quirked up on one side. "Well, my mom might disagree with you. I can't tell you the number of times she had to shush me as a kid. The thing she doesn't get is that she's just like me." Sasha laughed.

"No..." He feigned a surprised look.

She let go of one of his hands to swat at his arm. "Watch it, *monché*."

His heart was lighter than it had been in a long time. He loved sitting here sparring verbally with her. Loved the way she spoke her mind, no matter what her mom might have thought. Loved...her.

Hell. Had he just said that aloud?

No. Her eyes hadn't rounded in horror. She hadn't pulled back in disgust. He'd only voiced the words in his head. But it was enough. Enough to set them in concrete.

Was it possible?

She did tend to say what she thought. So,

unlike his parents, she was easier to read. Easier to get a straight answer from. Something else that he liked. Suddenly he wanted his parents to meet her. Wanted them to see how different Sasha was from them.

"I think you're right about my mom and dad. I'm going to invite them. Whether they like what we've done with the clinic or not is immaterial. But they deserve to see where my trust fund has gone and that it's doing good things. That whether or not they care, the money they put into that fund is helping others."

Sasha smiled again. "I think that's a very good thing. You're not responsible for what they think or don't think. You're only responsible for you."

For once he believed that. Believed in the possibility of something outside the walls he'd built around his heart.

His fingers found her cheek. "Come back to my apartment, Sash."

"Are we having drinks? I drove my car here."

His thoughts were spiraling way too fast for him to keep up with. Before he quite realized what was happening, he said, "What if you just left your car here all night and picked it up in the morning?"

Her eyes came up and found his. "Leave it here in front of the clinic?"

"Yes."

"And pick it up in the…"

He nodded.

Her smile was slow in coming, but when it appeared, it lit up her whole face. "Why, Dr. Edwards, are you asking me to spend the night with you?"

"Would you say yes, if I were?"

"Mmm, let me think…"

Just when he thought she was going to come up with some excuse about needing to be at work the next day or telling him it wouldn't be a good idea, she gifted him with a kiss on the palm of his hand.

"I say yes."

There was no road leading back to the housing complex, just a wide sandy path set with bamboo torches. Since it was early afternoon, the lights hadn't come on yet. "Are these gas lamps?"

"No. Electric. I didn't want any danger of something catching on fire."

He took her hand and twined his fingers in hers as they walked. She needn't have worried about anyone seeing them, since it looked like the area was deserted. "Do all of the clinic staff live here?"

"Not all. Some of the doctors do, but some of the other staff members already have housing in other parts of the island."

They came into a clearing of domiciles that were replicas of each other. But they were lovely. The outsides were painted in the same pale green tones as the inside of the hotel. It blended into the greenery around them. "How many homes are there?"

"Twenty right now. If we expand our staff at all, we'll have to add a few more."

Normally she might have balked at that, but the spots were so tastefully made, and it looked like they'd done their best to preserve the nature around them. "There are no cars back here?"

"No. We have a couple of golf carts that we can bring back here and the odd truck when someone moves in or out, but for the most part we just try to keep things quiet and peaceful."

"It really is." She scuffed at the path. "What would your mom think of all this sand?"

He laughed. "She would absolutely hate it."

They made it to the very back of the buildings, and around the corner there was only one house. And behind it was a stand of palm trees and low shrubbery. "This is yours?"

A hammock was stretched between two of the trees, and it wasn't just some tourist decoration. There was a plastic cup sitting on the ground beside it as if he'd used it very recently. She glanced up at him. Nate surprised her in a lot of different ways.

And it scared her just a little bit.

The sand turned to river rocks as they reached a small path leading up to his front door. A very practical way of losing the sand from your shoes as you walked toward the entryway. "This is beautiful."

"Thank you. I wanted the staff who live here to have a quiet place to come home to once they finish at the clinic."

"And you didn't want a nice quiet place to come to this afternoon?"

He used their still clasped hands to pull her against him. "No, not this afternoon. Maybe not even tonight."

She hadn't gotten to see all of him the last time they were together, but this time?

Her mouth watered at the thought. They would be totally alone. Totally cut off from any possibility of being caught, since his house wasn't attached to any of the others. She assumed there were wives and children in here somewhere, but right now, it was quiet, as if this were their own little oasis of space.

And in a very real sense it was true. Someone would have to purposely skirt some obstacles to get back to his home.

As if reading her thoughts, his arms went around her waist and he walked her backward, up the rock path, under the overhang, against the front door. The wood was solid and smooth against her back, the cool surface a welcome contrast to the heat radiating off his body.

He propped his forearms on either side of her, leaning in, touched his nose to hers. "Are you wearing them?"

His fresh breath washed over her face, and she shivered at how close he was. How his words were making her squirm against him. "Wearing what?"

He dipped closer, his cheek brushing hers as he moved to her ear. "The same panties?"

Confusion went through her until she realized what he was talking about. The underwear from their other encounter. "I can't remember."

She remembered very well, but wasn't going to stand here and describe them. They weren't the same pair, but they were from the same maker. A silky black undergarment cut deep in the back. And she wanted him to slide them slowly down her legs.

His mouth moved across hers, a light touch that drove her crazy with need, one leg coming between hers and pressing hard against her.

That felt so good. Familiar. Her arms went around his neck, as she tilted her head to deepen the kiss. Except he pulled away.

"Nate?"

"I don't want it out here. And if I keep kissing you, that's exactly what's going to happen."

"Mmm, does it matter?"

He leaned back and pulled his lanyard over his head, reaching beside her to press the key card to something. The door clicked open suddenly, and if he hadn't been holding her, she would have fallen through the entryway. As it was, the momentum caused them both to lurch through it, Sasha giving a slight shriek as she almost tumbled backward.

Somehow they stayed upright, Nate kicking the door shut behind them.

He said something and lights came on around them. He must have an automated wireless system, a luxury on most parts of the island. Something squelched inside her, but she pushed it back as he kissed her again.

Soon, her thoughts zeroed back in on the man and his palms sliding down her arms, her loose sleeveless dress rippling against her body as his fingers touched portions of it. "Let me take my shoes off," she murmured against his mouth.

He stood and watched as she kicked her white thong-style sandals off on the tiled floor. The flooring extended into the living room where pale sand-colored walls gave the place an open, spacious feeling. Then his arms were back around her. "Are you hungry?"

"No."

"Thirsty?"

She smiled. "No."

He leaned down until his arms were just under her bottom and he picked her up so that her face was at the same level as his. "Good." He kissed her, walking with her to some back part of the house. Down a short hallway and through another door.

His bedroom.

He walked over to a massive carved four-poster bed and turned to sit down, her feet touching the floor. She didn't wait for an invitation; she scrambled onto the bed, her legs straddling his hips, her hands cupping the back of his head.

"Hi," she whispered.

He kissed her. "Hi yourself."

She could feel him against her, hard and ready, and they'd barely touched. It made her smile, because it matched the ache that was growing inside her, waiting for him. How could that be?

It had been very different with Austin. Something she didn't want to think about right now.

Nate bunched her dress in his hands, sliding it up her thighs as she raised up a bit to help. Then it was around her waist and she was that much closer to him. His fingers explored her underwear and she shivered as his palms smoothed over the skin he found at the edges of the elastic.

God, she wanted to be next to him without any barriers between them. She reached down and found the hem of her dress, pulled it up and over her head, tossed it onto the far side of the mattress.

When she reached behind her to unhook her bra, he stopped her. "Let me."

He found the clasp and the rush of air against her back was a heady experience. Closer. She needed to be closer to him.

As if reading her mind he dragged off his polo shirt, letting it drop to the floor in the same spot he'd discarded her bra.

She couldn't help herself. She mashed herself against his chest, her nipples instantly hardening at the unexpected friction from the dusting of hair she found there.

One of his hands slid up her back in a steady move until he reached her nape, fingers sinking deep into her hair.

"Hell, Sash. I didn't think anything could be better than last time, but…"

She understood exactly what he meant. "I know."

His lips pressed against the side of her neck, trailing up and over her jaw, peppering tiny kisses along her cheek until he was back at her mouth. Then he was right where he needed to be, teeth and tongue and mouth devouring hers in a way that made her breathless and so very needy.

She squirmed against him, lifting and sliding in a way that mimicked what she wanted to happen. Needed to happen.

When she couldn't stand it anymore, she climbed off him, her lips leaving his as he groaned.

"Just a minute," she whispered. "I need to…"

She stripped off her underwear, as Nate's eyes followed her every move. "I can't believe you're here with me."

"I am. I'm right here."

Then she reached for his trousers and popped the button free.

CHAPTER ELEVEN

NATE WAS ON fire as Sasha tugged his pants down his hips, taking his boxers with them. Then he was free, the air from the room sluicing over him like the waves in the sea.

"Come here." His voice was rougher than he'd meant it to be, but she evidently didn't mind, because she just laughed.

"Not quite yet." She pulled something from the back pocket of his slacks and tossed it to him. "New wallet?"

"Yes." He took it and opened it to where he'd put a new packet, took it out and then tossed the wallet onto his night table. He started to tear it open, but she stopped him.

He looked at her in puzzlement, until she pulled him to his feet and turned him to face the bed, while she slowly sat on it. She reached her hand out for the condom, but when he gave it to her, she set it on the bed next to her hip.

"I thought this might be just the perfect height. And I was right." Her smile held a secret knowledge.

He had no idea what she was talking about, until her hands reached for him and drew him slowly toward her.

Hell! The second her mouth slid over him, he wondered if it was all over. The wet heat took him by storm, destroying his defenses. He buried his hands in her hair in an attempt to gain some semblance of control over the situation. But it wasn't happening. Sasha was doing what Sasha did, being as direct with her actions as she was with her words. He loved it. Feared it. Wanted it more than anything he knew.

All he could do was somehow show her. His fingers stroked her face, brushed her hair off her forehead even as his eyes closed and he allowed himself to take in every sensation she let him have.

There was no sense of selfishness in this woman. No taking whatever she could get. And he was coming very close to…

His eyes opened with a start and he pulled free. "No. Not like this."

She sat back on the bed, licking her lips with a smile. "What? You didn't like it?" She reached for him again. "I could just finish—"

"It's my turn." He ripped open the condom and slid it over himself before bearing her down onto the bed and covering her body with his. "God, I want you so much it hurts."

It was true. His body ached. But so did his chest. His eyes. Parts of him that he never equated with sex. Because it wasn't just about sex. This was his first time making love and knowing that it actually was about more than just the physical act. So he showed her. Loved her. And when he finally parted her legs and entered her, it was a spiritual experience. A sharing he'd never experienced with any other woman.

Sasha wrapped her legs around him, like she had in the water, but the solidness of the bed held them up without them needing to put any effort into that part. Instead, he could just concentrate on the push and pull of their bodies as the inner waves began to build.

And when she breathed his name, he knew it was time. Reaching between them, he found that sensitive spot that he knew she liked. Stroked it, teased it, while kissing her and whispering how much he wanted her, how good it felt to be inside her. How he needed to feel her let go against him.

He quickened his pace, their bodies tangled together in a heap that he hoped he could never unravel. He thrust harder, touched her with more urgency until she was arching against him, gasping for him not to stop. He didn't. Drove home with all he had.

And then he felt her give way beneath him, her hips moving frantically as she came. He could hold back no longer, pouring everything he had into her with a fury that surprised him. He buried his face against her neck and rode out wave after wave of sensation, trying to draw it out as his pumping got slower, less frantic.

Then he was still, enjoying the feeling of being joined with her in the soft aftermath, as her hands stroked up and down his back.

Surely she'd felt what he'd felt. He opened his mouth to say the words, but something stoppered them in the back of his throat. He wasn't sure what it was. Or why.

This was all happening too fast. They'd known each other what? A few weeks?

She'd had one terrible relationship; he didn't want to do anything that might scare her off. So maybe it was best just to let things ride. They could take it slow. He could take her to the gala as his date.

Introduce her to his parents.

Was he kidding? They didn't even come into the equation when it came to Sasha.

He felt her shift beneath him and realized a lot of his weight was on her.

"Sorry." He rolled off her, only to have her come onto her side, her fingers playing in the hair of his chest.

"Don't be. That was…delicious."

He laughed. Leave it to her to come up with a term that was so unexpected, and yet so perfect. It was why he lo… No. Don't jinx it. Take it slow, remember? "It was, was it?"

He dragged her on top of him, kissing her, then smoothing her hair back so he could look into her face. "Now, I'm hungry. So I'll fix us something to eat. Then," he slid his mouth down the side of her jaw, "then, once it's good and dark, and the rest of the world is in bed, I want to take you outside and rock you to sleep in that hammock that's sitting under the trees."

She bit his lip. "And if I don't want to go to sleep?"

"Oh, sweetheart. The sleeping won't take place for a very long time."

Sasha didn't wake up in the hammock. But true to his word, he had rocked her to sleep out there. Her face heated at all the things they'd done out in the open air. She had no idea you could do that many things in a rocking bed. A flash of worry went through her that she quickly banished. It didn't mean he'd learned those things with some other woman.

The thought of him spending time in that hammock with someone else made her slightly nauseous. Maybe because of the way it molded to your body in a way that a mattress didn't. It was close and intimate, and so very sexy.

Don't think about it.

She turned her head to find him already awake, his hair wet from a recent shower. He was lying on the bed propped on his elbow watching her. And he smelled divine.

It made her feel kind of sweaty and grimy and she wasn't sure why.

And when he smiled and bent down to kiss her, she ducked out of the way. "I haven't brushed my teeth yet."

"I don't care."

She laughed. "Well, I do. It's not fair for you to be all clean and fresh. Let me get a shower, then we'll talk."

"Okay. First I want to ask you something."

Something about the way he said that made her blink. "What is it?"

"It's about the gala."

She relaxed. "Can't it wait until after I

shower?" For some reason, she really needed to be on an equal footing with him.

"Sure. I'll get you a towel." He got off the bed and waited until she'd scrambled off as well before moving out of the room. Now that she could actually look around without the thrill of kisses and distractions of love-making, she was surprised by how large the room was. It was probably twice the size of her bedroom. She wasn't sure why that felt important, but it did.

She fidgeted and then looked for her clothes, not finding them. "Nate?"

He reappeared holding a thick beige towel. Her clothes were folded neatly on top of it.

"Did you wash these?" Austin had never done anything like that. It would have never even crossed his mind. But somehow it made her feel guilty. How long had Nate been up?

"It was no problem. There is shampoo and soap in the bathroom. Help yourself."

"Thank you." She padded to the bathroom that she'd briefly seen between lovemaking sessions and closed the door behind her. The decor was in keeping with the island feel, but it was well-appointed, just like his bedroom. And the curved faucets were pricey.

She frowned. *Why does it matter, Sasha?* Nate wasn't pretentious. At all. In fact, the fancy decor seemed a little out of character with the Nate she'd grown accustomed to. Maybe these apartments also served to house families of patients in case the hotel filled up, like he said happened during the gala.

That made sense. She relaxed and turned on the shower, allowing the warm water to flow over her body and soothe the slight aches of muscles that she hadn't noticed last night. Nate was certainly...active...in his lovemaking. But, *oh* it had been wonderful and almost overwhelming.

She soaped her hair and then let the water sluice over it, rinsing the suds. She smiled. She was going to smell like him.

No, not like him. Because there was no scent known to man that could smell as good as he did. Her hands trailed down her stomach, shivering as she remembered his touch. His body covering hers.

Oh, she was getting worked up all over again. She needed to get out of here and get home. Where she could unpack everything that had happened last night.

Finishing up, she turned the taps off and stepped out of the shower onto the thick mat. After toweling herself dry, she wrapped the towel around her hair, while she got dressed. Glancing at the bathroom vanity, she frowned again when she spied a new toothbrush wrapped in cellophane and a tiny tube of toothpaste next to it. Also new and unused.

The thoughts of him bringing other women here slithered back into her head. For once, she wished she carried a toothbrush in her purse so she could leave those on the counter untouched. But she didn't, so she ripped open the package and brushed her teeth as quickly as she could, rinsed her mouth. She held the toothbrush there for a minute and looked at the holder where he kept his.

No way.

She went over to the small stainless-steel trash can and stepped on the lever to open it. Then she tossed the brush and toothpaste into it.

She wasn't sure what she was getting so uneasy about. It was a nice gesture. Just like washing her clothes.

But then she thought she'd known Austin too. Except he'd never showered her with these little touches either. She unwrapped her hair and dragged her fingers through it, arranging the curls the best she could. Thank heavens he hadn't set out a new hairbrush, as well.

She looked at herself in the mirror. The

woman staring back at her looked wide-eyed and unsure of herself. She recognized that person from another time in her life and quickly turned her back on her.

Gathering her composure, she counted to ten before opening the bathroom door and re-entering the bedroom. Nate was nowhere to be seen now. Thank goodness. But she was going to have to face him sometime.

The smell of bacon and eggs reached her nose and her stomach took a swan dive. She had no idea what was wrong with her. She had not felt like this the first time they made love. But they hadn't been in his house, where the trappings of luxury surrounded her. It had just been her and Nate and the ocean. And she'd felt on equal footing with him.

She didn't want to sit at a table with china plates and try to think of what she could say to him. But if he'd made her breakfast, she didn't very well see how she could refuse without hurting his feelings. And really, he'd done nothing wrong. He was still the same person he'd been when he'd first come to Saint Victoria Hospital that day.

So she moved into the living area and forced a cheerful smile on her face. "Good morning."

He came around from the kitchen, his feet bare, wearing dark jeans and an unbuttoned shirt. The dusting of hair on his chest narrowed and slid in a smooth trail past his waistband.

. This man was any girl's fantasy. And maybe he was.

"Safe to kiss now?"

What could she say? No? She held her face up and his lips brushed across hers, familiar and warm. Her uneasiness subsided a bit.

"Everything okay?" he asked.

"Fine. It's a little later than I expected."

He glanced back at the stainless-steel clock over his sink. It matched the rest of the appliances. "It's barely six."

"I know, but I kind of want to head home before a lot of other people are up."

A frown puckered his brow, but he nodded. "Of course."

"Oh, you wanted to ask me something about the gala. Is it about my mom? As far as I know she has everything under control. I'll be there helping her serve, of course, along with a whole slew of other people."

"You're planning on serving?"

"Yes, why?"

He paused as if trying to figure out a way

to say something. "Does she not have enough help?"

"I'm sure she does, but she's my mom, and I want to pitch in."

The slithering thoughts about him being here with other women morphed and changed into something else. "Is there a problem with that?"

"No. I just thought it might be nice if a member of each of our hospitals greeted the guests. I was going to ask you if you would be Saint Victoria Hospital's representative."

"And who would be the clinic's representative?"

"I would be."

Memories of her time with Austin resurfaced, ugly and eerily similar. He had cared about where they went for dinner, what she wore, one time even buying her a dress to wear to an opera he wanted to go to.

So Nate didn't want her serving food to his rich guests? The nausea that had disappeared with his kiss resurfaced. Would the Nate wearing a tuxedo at his gala be a total stranger to her? Would he wander regally from group to group asking if they had everything they needed while her mom and the rest of her crew waited hand and foot on them?

Suddenly she didn't want to find out. Knew now why she'd avoided going to the gala in the past. She'd already visited in the circles of the very wealthy during her time with Austin, and in the end found out that it was nothing like its glitzy facade. What she'd seen of Austin's world was shallow and entitled, and the people were used to having things handed to them.

Sasha was used to working her ass off for everything she'd accomplished. Did she regret her time at Harvard? No. The school had been wonderful, and she was truly grateful for being gifted with that education. It had allowed her to do what she loved most in this world. But she couldn't bear it if Nate turned out to be exactly like the man she'd once imagined him to be, the man she'd been avoiding for the last three years.

"Nate, I can't. I'm sorry. I told my mother I was going to help her, and that's where I need to be. I'm sure the hospital administrator over at Saint Victoria Hospital, or any number of people would be happy to help you greet your guests."

His frown deepened. "I understand."

But he didn't. She could see it in his face. Sense it in the stiff formal posture he'd settled into. This was wrong. She never should have come here. Should have left things as they were with the rosy image of what they'd had that day on the beach.

She found her sandals in the entryway and somehow managed to stuff her feet into them, even though her eyes were gritty and difficult to see through. "I really do need to get home, Nate—I'm sorry I can't stay for breakfast."

"I'll walk you to your car."

"No!" If she had to travel down that sandy path with him, she wasn't going to make it without bursting into tears. History really did repeat itself, and Sasha was finding out just how stupid she was for believing the distance between them could be spanned. It couldn't. Her heart was sitting there telling her it was possible, but her mind… Her mind was telling her what she'd known all along. She and Nate were on different courses. A geometry term popped into her mind and she grabbed at it.

Asymptotes.

They were asymptotes. He was a line and she was a curve that got closer and closer to him, but never quite reached where he was. She would never be a part of that world. Didn't even want to.

It was better that she found out now than

later, when her emotions had become too tangled up in him.

Weren't they already?

Oh, she hoped not. Couldn't bear it if she actually fell for him.

A whispering in her mind circled around, but she chased it away, horrified when she realized her hands had actually gone up and followed the thought.

"Sasha, what is it?"

His voice came through a fog, but she was shaking her head telling him she was fine, she just had some things she needed to do. Without waiting for him to say anything else, she fled out his door, hurried down the sandy path and somehow made it to her car.

Once there, she buried her head in her arms against the steering wheel and cried until there were no more tears. Thank the Lord he hadn't followed her. And since it was still really early, there was no one around to see her start her car, back out of the parking spot and head down the road. Away from The Island Clinic. Away from Nate.

In her rearview mirror, the bronze likeness of Marie stared mournfully after her, arms outstretched as if pleading with her not to go. But she had to. For her own self-preservation. And to hold on to what good memories she still had of her and Nate's time together. Because she knew deep down, there was no chance of it ever happening again. She would make sure of it.

Nate sat at his desk, toying with his cell phone, before finally tossing the thing into a drawer. He hadn't seen Sasha in a week. He'd tried calling her, but he was always sent straight to voice mail. And the two times he'd driven over to Saint Victoria Hospital, he'd been told by Patty, a friend of hers, that she was in surgery and she had no idea when she would be out.

He finally got the message. She was avoiding him. He wasn't sure why. Unless she'd sensed that he cared for her, and she didn't return his feelings. The look on her face when he'd asked her to stand with him to greet guests had sent a chill over him. She'd looked...stricken. That was the only word he could come up with to describe it. Was it that repugnant to her to actually be seen with him in public?

He swallowed. Why not? His parents had pretty much avoided being seen with him once he told them he wasn't interested in joining their practice.

Well, damn.

It wasn't like he hadn't been through this before. He should be well used to it by now. But Sasha had seemed so caring and understanding when he'd talked about his devastation over losing Marie, and when he'd shared from his heart about his parents and how hurt he'd been by their behavior.

Had it all been an act?

Again. Why not?

She'd been quick to offer her mom's services when she'd come to that meeting about the gala. She'd been there what, ten minutes, and then her hand went up and she asked why they didn't use local businesses.

But she'd slept with him after he offered the catering to her mom. There was no way those two things could be connected. Could they?

He didn't think so, but his mind was so screwed up right now that he was no longer sure of anything.

Dammit all. This was why he didn't do relationships anymore. He had no idea what was what…what was true and what wasn't, when it came to other people's emotions. Or his own.

Well, he wasn't going to call her again. If she didn't want to talk to him, then so be it. If she didn't want to stand beside him, that was all well and good. To prove that point, he called Saint Victoria Hospital and got hold of Maurice, the hospital administrator—he refused to believe it was because that was who Sasha had suggested—and found the man was more than willing to help him in that endeavor. So even if she came back and offered, he'd tell her he already had it covered.

She wouldn't though. He knew it in his soul. When she'd walked out of his apartment, she'd done so with the intention of never coming back. And he had no idea why.

But he hadn't begged his parents not to turn their backs on him all those years ago, and he wasn't going to beg Sasha not to do so now. He just didn't have it in him. Not today. And probably not tomorrow, either.

When he saw her at the gala tomorrow night, maybe he'd get a better sense of what was going on with her. He'd just wait and see if her attitude changed. Maybe she just needed time to process what had happened at his place.

But something told him otherwise.

Well, hell, he didn't have time to worry about this. Not with the fund-raiser already on his doorstep. He took Marie's doll down from the shelf and set her on his desk. This was what he needed to keep in front of him.

This was his entire reason for coming to Saint Victoria. It hadn't been for Sasha or his parents or anyone else. It had been because of the way a young child had touched his heart and challenged him to make a difference.

That motivation had been enough years ago.

And it would be enough to get him through the next day or week or year.

CHAPTER TWELVE

"WHAT DO YOU MEAN, you don't feel well? Do you have a fever?"

Sasha stood at her door in pajamas and shook her head at her mom. There was no way she could go to that gala. She thought she could. Thought she could hold her head up high and face Formal Nate, all decked out in his finest garb. But she couldn't.

"Sasha, you're scaring me. Did you get the results back from the test?"

She'd convinced her uncle Art to tell her mom about his illness, but there was a string attached. She had to come clean about the genetic test she'd taken.

But she wished now that she'd waited until after the gala was over. Her mom had been obsessed and worried and had almost said she couldn't do the catering. Sasha had panicked and begged her to please go through with it. It would mean a lot to the island

and a lot to her. Besides, her mom needed something to keep her mind off things she couldn't control.

"I didn't. But this has nothing to do with amyloidosis. My stomach is just in knots. It was a hard day at work, and I'm exhausted." That last part was a lie, but the part about her stomach was very true. But it was in knots from nerves and heartache over what had happened with Nate. She probably should have taken his calls and just come clean about her feelings, but the grinding sense of despair had kept her from doing that. She hadn't wanted to believe the worst about Austin, only to find out it was very true. It crushed her to think that Nate might be cut from the very same cloth.

Wasn't it better to assume, thereby avoiding having the actual facts slap her right in the face?

She didn't know, but she was running on fumes right now, and the gala wasn't the place to tackle those hard questions. Maybe after it was over, she'd make an appointment to see him.

Make an appointment.

God, she'd made love to the man, and yet she didn't have the courage to march into his office and tell him she needed to ask him a question. Whether or not he was the person she hoped he was, or whether he was the person she feared he was.

"Is this about Nate?" Her mom's voice cut through her musings like a knife, slashing into emotions that were already raw.

"What? Of course not."

Her mom stared at her, then grabbed her arms and led her over to the sofa. "Oh, honey, tell me. Are you afraid of the diagnosis?"

Sasha couldn't suppress a laugh that quickly turned to a gasping sob. She hadn't been. It hadn't even crossed her mind since that day at his cottage. Until now. And no matter how many times she'd told herself otherwise—told herself to think rationally—it was like one more nail hitting the coffin containing her hopes and dreams. She somehow got hold of herself. "No. That's not it."

"Then what?"

How could she say the actual words? She couldn't, so she simply said, "He's rich."

Tessi looked into her face. "Oh, honey. Nate is not Austin."

The bottom of her chin trembled as she took in those words. "But what if he is?" The question came out in whispered tones.

"I can't answer that question. All I can do is tell you to search your heart. Deep down, you know the truth. But until you believe it, until you pull it into your soul and hold it tight, you're not going to listen to what anyone says." She patted her cheek. "I have to go. But think about it. What I will say is don't wait too long to come to a conclusion. Because you might just find out you missed a chance at something that doesn't come along every day. Something like I had with your dad."

With that, Tessi stood. "I need to get going. Call me if you need anything. I'll answer, even if it's in the middle of the gala." With that she let herself out the door, going to the very place where Sasha should be going.

Nate spotted Tessi over by one of the long banquet tables setting out hors d'oeuvres. He went over to her. When she saw him, she put the lid on the tray she was holding and smiled. "Your guests will be arriving soon."

"Everything looks wonderful—thank you so much." He hesitated. "Is Sasha here? She mentioned she would be helping you serve tonight."

"No." She fixed him with a look. "She was feeling under the weather and decided to stay home."

That wasn't like Sasha. If he knew anything about her, it was that she was serious about her commitments. Was that why she'd run off like she had the last morning they were together? Was she afraid of being pressed to make a commitment she wouldn't be able to keep? Well, she wouldn't have to worry about that anymore. He wasn't going to press her for anything.

"Is it something serious?"

"I'm sorry, but I need to get back to the catering."

Real worry crawled down his spine. "Tessi, what's wrong with her?"

She looked at him for a minute, then shook her head. "That's not for me to say." She started to walk away, then stopped and turned to face him. "Do you think there's a difference between those of us who are here to serve food and those who come to eat that food?"

He frowned, not sure what she was saying. "No. Of course not."

She smiled. "That's all I needed to hear." With that she turned and moved to another long serving table, her hands working over it with a grace and elegance that reminded him of her daughter's hands as she'd stitched up their accident patient.

He had no idea what she'd meant by her

question, but sensed it was important. Critical. And that it had something to do with Sasha.

Do you think there's a difference between those of us who are here to serve food and those who come to eat that food?

Sasha had told him she was going to help her mom serve the food. And when he'd asked her to help him greet guests, instead, something in her face had changed. A wariness had come over her. When he'd pressed her, she'd bolted.

Why?

He stood there, his mind mulling Tessi's words until they were burned into his brain.

Then something sliced through him like a hemostatic scalpel, cutting and cauterizing as it went. And he knew what was wrong. At least he thought he did.

Austin.

The rich boyfriend she'd had at Harvard who'd cast her aside after five years of dating. She'd said enough about him that Nate knew that relationship had wounded her deeply.

What had Sasha said to him one time? *I'm hoping I was wrong about you.* Nate had told her he hoped she was wrong too.

Maybe she'd taken his request for her

to greet guests the wrong way. He'd never meant to imply that helping her mom serve was any less important. Tessi was a smart woman. She'd asked him that question for a reason.

Hell, in trying to go slow, in trying to court her, he'd sent a message he'd never meant to send.

So what was he going to do about it?

He was going to go see her and confess to his real crime. That he loved her and had been too much of a coward to tell her that last night they were together. And if she kicked him out of her house?

Well, then he'd know he was wrong. That she really didn't love him. And he would accept it and go on. But there was no way he was giving up without at least trying.

He made his way back over to where Tessi stood. She glanced over at him as if she knew. And she smiled. "I forgot to say you look very nice. Very…*sophisticated*."

Nate took the heavy tray from her. "Where is she?"

"At home." Tessi rattled off an address that Nate committed to memory.

He then bent down and kissed her cheek. "Thank you for everything. For doing such a wonderful job here. And for teaching your daughter to be the incredible woman she is." He motioned to the tray. "Where do you want this?"

"Those happen to be extras. Why don't you find someone to share them with?"

He laughed. She was not very subtle. But then she was like her daughter. Direct. Sometimes blunt. But with a heart of gold. A heart he wasn't sure he deserved.

But he was damned well going to try to win it.

"Thanks for the food. I'll return the tray." He could not believe he was about to run out on a gala that could very well provide another year's worth of funding for both The Island Clinic and Saint Victoria Hospital. But Frank Seldridge had been his backup for the last two years and would do an admirable job of holding down the fort. He found his friend talking to one of the early arrivals. Nate greeted them with a smile, his chest tight with the need to get away, to go find Sasha.

He murmured to Frank, "I have somewhere I need to be. I really need you to step in for me tonight. Can you do it?"

The surgeon, who was well on the way to working a miracle on Merriam Blankenship, could perform just as big a miracle tonight.

The man took one look at the covered silver tray in Nate's hands and glanced up in his face. Whatever he read there must have convinced him. "Go. We'll be fine."

"Thanks."

"Oh, and Nate..." He chuckled. "Best of luck."

He appreciated it, because he was going to need it.

He hurried down the front steps, only to run smack-dab into his parents. He'd totally forgotten they were coming tonight. But he didn't have time for this right now.

"Nathaniel, how nice to see you," his father said. "Nice little place you have here."

Was he kidding? Before he had a chance to respond, his mom took him by the shoulders and gave him an air kiss on the cheek. "Why are you holding that tray, dear?"

Said as if everything between them was perfectly normal. Well, he wasn't going to stand around and chitchat. If they wanted to talk to him, they could get in line. Behind the person who meant more than anything in this world to him. "I'm taking some food to a...friend."

What else could he call her? He certainly didn't know if she was going to kick him out on his ass the second he showed up at her house.

He gave them both a smile that he hoped looked genuine enough and said, "I'm sorry. I'll talk to you later, but please stay and see what it is I've been up to for the last three years."

With that, he turned and headed out to the parking lot.

Nate drove as fast as he safely could, although the ride to Williamtown still seemed to take forever. But then he was entering the main street of the town, glancing at the address he'd scribbled onto a scrap of paper. He drove slowly down a side street that was less than a mile from the hospital. The white house was modest but neat, a tended garden out front boasting a colorful array of flowers, while a huge bougainvillea sprawled over an archway, behind which was a dark red door.

He felt a little stupid standing there in a tuxedo holding a silver tray. But he had a feeling words were not going to be enough right now. He knocked on the door.

He waited for a minute, wondering if she could see him and would refuse to open the door. Then he heard the sound of a lock snicking. The door opened.

Sasha stood there in an…evening gown? Then she tilted her head and stared at him, her glance trailing over him. "Nate? What are you doing here? You're supposed to be at the gala."

"I'm playing hooky."

"You're playing what?" Her eyes widened. "Is that my mother's tray?" Her hand went to her mouth, then a string of Creole words poured out, searing the air around them. "Did she *send* you here?"

"No, she didn't. And I won't ask you what you just said."

Her lips twitched the tiniest bit. "Good. Because you might not like the answer."

"Can I come in? Your mom's tray is rather heavy."

She glanced down at herself. "I was just getting ready to go to…"

He realized why she had the dress on. "You were coming?"

"Yes. I decided I had some unfinished business."

A flare of hope surged through him. Sasha stepped aside and let him in, directing him to set the tray on a pass-through counter that divided the living room from the kitchen.

"I like your house."

"Thanks."

The furnishings were clean and comfortable, and she had a flare for decorating. The room pulled you in and invited you to stay.

He realized how cold his own house might have appeared with its more formal furnishings. But the houses were all decorated alike, in case they needed to be pulled into service as extra places to house guests.

But looking at it after what he'd figured out, he could see how it might have seemed to Sasha. And his request that she greet guests... Hell. He wasn't sure how to make it right. Except she was dressed in formal wear, the green fabric of her dress hugging her slender curves to a tee. She said she'd been getting ready to come to the gala. That she had unfinished business.

With him?

She seemed to gather her composure. "Why are you here?"

"This is where I should be. Where I needed to be. But let me ask you this. Why are you here, rather than at the gala?"

"I was late in coming to a decision."

He took a step closer. "Care to tell me what that decision is?"

"I—I..."

Taking one of her hands in his, he said,

"Okay, I'll go first. I have something I need to tell you."

"You do?"

"Yes." He led her over to the couch. Then his gaze held hers as he prepared to pour out his heart and soul. "I don't know what you think of me, Sash, or what you think you know of me, but... I'm not rich."

"What?" Shock went through her face.

"It's true. I sank every penny of my trust fund into the clinic. I earn a salary as a doctor and as the chief of staff, but it's not a hefty one. Because that's not what I want. That's *not why I'm there*." He drew the words out very slowly.

"But your house..."

"It's a cookie-cutter house, made just like all the rest of them. We made everything to pull double duty, if necessary."

Her eyes traveled over his tuxedo, touching the collar, sliding over his bow tie. "You look very nice."

"So do you. But then you're beautiful no matter what you're wearing. Or not wearing." He smiled and took both her hands, doing his best not to get sidetracked this time. "I need you to know that even if I were wealthy. Even if I had all the money in the world, I would still want to be on this island, doing exactly what I'm doing. I would still be the same man who's sitting next to you right now."

"I figured that out just a little while ago. It's why I'd decided to come to the gala." Tears welled in her eyes. "I misjudged you again. I'm sorry, Nate."

"I realize now how I might have come across at the house. I wanted you to be with me to greet the guests because... I love you, Sasha. Not for any other reason."

"And I thought you—"

"I know."

"My mom?"

He paused. "Not exactly. She was careful not to say very much. But it was enough that I realized how my words might have come across. I promise—I want nothing more from you than a chance to be with you. For the long haul. Not just for five years." He let that sink in for a minute before going on. "Not for ten years. But for the rest of our lives."

She leaned against him, putting her head on his shoulder. "I feel like such a fool. My mom told me you were nothing like..."

"Austin?"

"I was so afraid to believe, to just listen to my heart."

"I know. Me too." He wrapped his arms around her, pulling her closer. "Looks like we both have some growing to do. As individuals. And as a couple."

"You never entertained other women at your house? The toothbrush, the toiletries?"

"All in case a guest needed to use the house unexpectedly. I would have vacated and slept in my office."

"Of course." She drew in a deep breath. "Can you forgive me?"

"There's nothing to forgive, although my parents seemed pretty peeved at my leaving them standing on the steps of the conference center."

She sat up and looked at him. "You didn't?"

"I did. And I don't regret it. If they really want to reconnect, they'll try again. If they don't, then…" He gave a shrug.

Her face got very still. "Wait. We can't. Not until I find out the results of my test."

"Do you really think that would change things?"

"It should. You don't have to—"

He stopped what she was going to say with a kiss. "Yes. I do. I love you. I don't want to live without you. That is, unless you don't…"

"I do. But then I'm sure my very discreet mother already let that cat out of the bag too."

"Actually, she didn't. But she did hint that

I might want to take that tray and make a beeline for your house."

Sasha laughed, the sound lighter and more carefree than anything he'd heard in a while. And it was sweeter than the finest symphony.

"Well, it's a good thing. Because if you hadn't, I would have stormed that gala and yelled at the top of my lungs until someone found you and brought you to me." She sighed. "I realized what a mistake I was making. I love you too, by the way."

"Thank God. And if you'd shown up, I would have been honored to have you standing by my side or to have you helping your mom with the catering. You're my other half, Sasha. The one I didn't realize I was missing."

"How about if neither of us goes to the gala. What if we both stay right here?"

"I like the way you think."

She toyed with his bow tie, giving it a playful tug. "Think they'll miss us?"

"It wouldn't matter if they do." He smiled at her. "Why? Do you have something in mind?"

This time the tug on his tie was serious and succeeding in loosening the knot enough that it hung free around his neck.

"I'm wondering how long it takes to get a very handsome man out of his tuxedo?"

He growled, pulling her toward him. "You'd better be talking about me."

"No one else, my love. No one else. I'll miss the hammock, but we'll have to make do with a bed that's a whole lot narrower than yours."

He kissed her long and hard. "Believe me, Sash. There's not going to be enough room between us to tell the difference." With that he scooped her into his arms and carried her into the interior part of the house. A place where they would pledge their love and become the asymptote that defied all the odds, when it dared to intersect and join lovers as one.

EPILOGUE

Two years later

NATE LOWERED HIS baby girl into her crib. "Good night, sweetheart."

She was already sound asleep, her belly full. He was finding he loved these middle-of-the-night feedings. It was a time when the world was still and quiet, when he could take the time to reflect on how utterly happy he was.

He reached into the pocket of his robe and felt something. Damn. He'd almost forgotten. He pulled the object free and walked over to the shelf that flanked the white crib. Placing the doll carefully in the spot he'd chosen, he touched its hand.

Arms encircled his midsection, and warm lips tickled his neck. "I have a lot to be grateful to her for."

Nate didn't ask who she meant; he knew. "It's still hard to think about her death."

"I know. But there's an awareness out there now, that our island is not exempt from things like schistosomiasis. And you're watching for it now. It won't take you by surprise again."

She was right. They'd treated three more cases over the last couple of years, all of them children. All of them had lived. Maybe Marie was somehow looking down on them, watching over her island and its inhabitants.

Sasha turned him around to face her. "Guess who I saw in town today?"

"Who?"

"Uncle Art."

Two years after his diagnosis, treatment had put him into remission. He would live with the condition for the rest of his life. But he was making the most of whatever time he had left.

"You did?"

"Yes. He was with Corinne."

He cocked his head, trying to place the name. "You mean *the* Corinne? The one whose parents broke them up?"

"Yep. And they looked pretty chummy." She reached up and cupped his face. "Wouldn't it be great if they got their happy ending too?"

"It would, indeed." Sasha's amyloidosis test had come back negative for the gene. They'd both been relieved, and while they'd already talked about having children, it had erased any lingering doubts. Dayna Marie Edwards had made her way into the world kicking and screaming and letting everyone know she was taking after her mama. She still was. Their baby was direct and to the point about what she needed and when she needed it. And Nate couldn't love her more. Couldn't love her mother more.

She glanced up at him. "Your mom called today. They booked their flight for next week."

Nate frowned. "Are you sure you're up to this?"

"I'm looking forward to it."

This would be his parents' third visit. The first time was at the gala, when he'd been too busy wooing Sasha to spend time with them. The second time was at their wedding a year ago. The fences weren't completely mended, but they were working on it. Thanks to Sasha's wisdom and her canny knack of moving chess pieces into just the right spot.

He still couldn't believe she was his. And he was hers. But he was never going to take her for granted. Never going to take their love for granted. They could have so easily lost it all.

But thank God they hadn't.

"Hey, come on." He leaned down to kiss her. "You need your sleep. I'm hoping she won't wake up again."

But if she did, Nate would come get her and bring her in to nurse so that Sasha wouldn't have to make the trek. It was the least he could do, and he did it with a grateful heart. He had the family he thought he'd never have.

The family who'd stolen his heart and then given it back. The family who showed him every single day how loved he was. And that was worth more than money to Nate.

It was…everything.

* * * * *

*Look out for the next story in the
The Island Clinic quartet*

Caribbean Paradise, Miracle Family
by Julie Danvers

*And there are two more tropical
stories to come
Available August 2021!*

*Also, if you enjoyed this story, check out
these other great reads from Tina Beckett*

**The Trouble with the Tempting Doc
Consequences of Their New York Night**

All available now!